One Strange Date

LAURENCE SHAMES

If I listen long enough to you,
I'd find a way to believe that it's all true...

Tim Hardin

DEDICATION

To Marilyn

...like breathing out and breathing in...

PROLOGUE

Renita Daughtry, twenty-two years old, was one of those increasingly rare people who had actually been born and raised in Key West.

To those who know only the raucous, ribald side of the Southernmost City—the spring break debauches, the festivals of nakedness--this might suggest that she must've grown up very fast and developed by her early twenties into a worldly or even jaded young woman. In fact the opposite was true.

Key West families tended to be very protective of their kids, especially their daughters, whom they quarantined as much as possible from the tourists' misbehavior and utter abdication of dignity. Duval Street was off-limits after dark; body-paint didn't count as clothing, and wet T-shirt contests were strictly for anonymous visitors. Local families, even those who themselves tended toward drinking and brawling and occasional adultery, usually went to church and sent their children to Catholic school if they could afford it. Local kids rode in yellow school busses and often dressed in uniforms; they played sports, went out for cheerleading. It was as if they lived in a quite normal, fairly wholesome but subtly fenced-off precinct of Gomorrah.

So Renita had grown up sheltered, and also with a vague but nagging sense of missing out on something, though she didn't know exactly what. The world she lived in was a very small one—not just an island, but an island within an island. Perhaps it was this dual sense of geographical and social boundaries that had made her a dreamy teenager. Not shy, exactly, just inward and distracted. She read a lot. She fantasized a lot. In her mind she visited faraway places and found herself confronted with many novel situations, most of them romantic and wonderful, a few of them dark, scary, and of course forbidden; and strangely exciting for those very reasons. The sometimes edgy tone of her daydreams, in turn, made her extremely curious about how her own mind and emotions worked, and back when she was eighteen, she'd decided that she wanted to go away to college and study Psychology.

She applied to Florida State, up in Tallahassee. Her parents didn't understand why she wanted to go so far away from home and were more than slightly hurt. But Renita, quietly determined, was accepted and she went.

By her junior year, her attachments to Key West had inevitably dwindled. Never very sociable, she'd drifted out of touch with her few old friends, most of whom were already settling into jobs or attending Keys Community. Among family, the only one she still spoke to regularly was her favorite uncle, Uncle Ralph.

Uncle Ralph had no children of his own, and therefore he'd never gotten into the habit of talking differently to kids. This was part of what Renita loved about him. He didn't talk down to her, he didn't judge. When he asked her a question, he actually listened hard and with an open mind to the answer. So his niece confided in him about things she discussed with no one else. How hard it was to get used to living in a bigger city. How awkward she felt trying to meet new people and how lonely she felt much of the time. How tempting it was to go running home, to retreat into the tiny, island life she'd been raised for, and how disappointed in herself she'd be if she gave in to that. Uncle Ralph had no magic words to give her but he always paid attention and he was always kind.

One day in April, as one of their leisurely phone chats was winding down, Renita said she had to go, she had a paper due.

"What's it on?" her uncle asked. He didn't want to keep her from her schoolwork but he was impressed, almost awed, by the range of things she studied.

"This weird thing called the Stockholm Syndrome. Ever hear of it?"

"No."

"It's when captives—hostages, whatever—start sympathizing with their captors. Seeing things their way. Sometimes even falling in love with them."

"Wait," said Uncle Ralph. "Someone takes a woman hostage and they fall in love?"

"Happens," said Renita.

"That's bizarre."

"Bizarre, not bizarre, it happens. It's psychology."

Gallantly, indignantly, Uncle Ralph said, "But he's captured her. He's stolen her!"

"That's how it looks from the outside," his niece said calmly. "I wonder how it looks to her."

"How could it look? It looks like she's been stolen."

"Right. Okay. But stolen from what? Say she didn't much like the life she'd had before. Say she felt trapped in it. Someone comes along, someone totally different from anyone she's ever known, and takes her away from it, offers her the possibility, at least, of a completely different life. Is he stealing her or freeing her?"

Uncle Ralph couldn't pinpoint the moment when the conversation had begun upsetting him, but by now he realized he was getting pretty worked up. "But it's wrong! It's against her will!"

"Is it? That's where it gets interesting. That's what I'm writing my paper about. I think maybe it's just a reflex to see the hostage as a victim, especially if it's a woman. This captor/captive business, maybe it isn't so one-sided. Maybe it's more complicated. More of a game. A dance, even."

"A dance?" Uncle Ralph felt he should say more but couldn't find the words. Something just sounded wrong to him, askew, maybe even dangerous, and he regretted that he himself hadn't gone to college and learned how to discuss things more calmly and persuasively.

His niece knew him pretty well and could tell from his silence that he was unsettled. Breezily, she said, "Hey, Uncle Ralph, it's just a college paper. I'm angling for a good grade, that's all. But listen, I gotta go." Then she added casually but not without a glistening note of coyness, "Gotta get it finished before I fly down to Naples."

"Naples? You're going to Naples?"

"Day after tomorrow. In a private jet. On a date."

Ralph, her uncle, not her parent, tried hard to sound enthusiastic and to keep any hint of worry or disapproval out of his voice. "Private jet, wow! That's a fancy date."

"I'll say."

"How well you know this guy?"

"Oh, not very. Not yet."

"Another one of these online things?"

"He sounds amazing," Renita said. "Lives a whole different kind of life. I'll tell you more next time we talk. Gotta go for now."

PART ONE

1.

Bert the Shirt d'Ambrosia, retired Mafioso, aged ninety-plus but still a snappy dresser, had long ago stopped chasing trouble. Trouble, though, by long habit, had never yet stopped chasing him. Trouble somehow managed to find him even in the most unlikely places. Safe places, quiet places, places that were generally considered havens or even sanctuaries of simplicity and peace.

Not long ago, trouble caught up with Bert on Smathers Beach.

It was just before sunset on a gorgeous Key West day in mid-April, a day to be savored because, as every longtime local could sense in his bones, it was probably one of the few mild ones remaining before the wilting heat and draining humidity of summer set in, before the wind died and the clouds swelled and sagged like pregnant bellies and the crisp line of the horizon melted into a soupy smudge. But on this day there was still a breeze that lifted shallow corduroy ripples in the green water and carried a bracing smell of dry seashells and iodine. What few clouds there were, were bright and cheerful and seemed thumbtacked to the sky.

Wanting to make the most of this rare day, Bert had cut short his gin rummy game at the Paradiso condo and headed across the street to the beach a bit earlier than usual. In his left hand he carried a folding beach chair with an aluminum frame and yellow plastic webbing. In his right hand he carried his chihuahua, Nacho.

Nacho was wearing tiny sunglasses with blue reflective lenses. Bert was wearing a loose-weave pullover in a color like that of orange sherbet; anticipating the relative cool of evening, he also toted in the crook of his arm a terry-cloth cabana jacket with a slightly faded print in a shuffleboard motif.

Tourist season was mostly over and the beach was not crowded. Easter had passed the week before; that year's spring break was already a fading memory of scooter noise and crushed beer cans and young bodies twitching with rampant urges. Bert picked his way carefully over the imported sand that the Tourist Board trucked in from the mainland every autumn and which had worn thin by every spring, showing the hard knuckles of ancient coral that underlay it. He carried his chair and his dog to his favorite spot—a place where the beach scalloped ever so slightly and bowed almost imperceptibly toward the south and west— and then he sat down. He adjusted the dog's sunglasses, making sure the earpieces weren't pinching the creature's outsized ears.

"Comfortable?" he asked the dog.

The dog nuzzled the old man's hand with its shiny black nose and licked at the dry and papery skin between his fingers.

Bert settled in and looked around. There were a few people in the water, mostly wading in just deep enough to pee. Some guys were throwing a football, very wobbly spirals. Joggers ran by, looking extremely serious, even solemn.

He'd been sitting there a while and the sun had gotten very low when a shadow fell across him. It was odd how often this happened, even on an uncrowded beach: People were oblivious about standing in someone else's light, blocking his view of the sunset, though they sure didn't like it when another person did it to them.

The old man squinted toward the figure standing between

him and the horizon. With the backlighting, all he could make out was the silhouette of a very well-built young man, buff but not bulky, shirtless, in a bathing suit that didn't cover much. Softly, amicably, Bert called out, "Excuse me."

The young man didn't seem to hear. Maybe he was deep in thought. Maybe it was because of the hiss of the wavelets as they spilled onto the shoreline and percolated down through sand.

"Excuse me," Bert said again, a bit louder.

Still no response. The sun was hovering an inch above the ocean.

"Yo, Muscles!" Bert shouted.

At that the young man turned around and that's when the trouble started. Two very large guys, dressed in street clothes and Ray-Bans and black pointy shoes, and unnoticed by Bert until that very instant, had been walking quickly up the beach at the water's edge. When the muscular young man swiveled around to face the person who'd called to him, he turned away from the other two, and they jumped him.

The beating was very brutal and extremely efficient. It happened in less time than it took for the sun to graze the horizon. One guy blindsided the young man with a ferocious punch to the kidney. As the victim crumpled and leaned away from the thump and sear of the blow, the other assailant kneed him to the side of the head and he went down on all fours just at the foamy edge of the Atlantic. The first guy kicked him in the ribs. Sand flew from his shoe and sprinkled the young man's sagging back. For good measure, the other thug tossed a handful of beach into his eyes and mouth.

Then it was over. Just like that.

The two attackers turned and walked away, quickly but without any unseemly hint of fleeing. The hurt man stayed down on his hands and knees, flexing his spine as though in a yoga pose, spitting out sand, chuffing like a dolphin as he tried to get his breath back. The chihuahua, in a spontaneous act of compassion, leaped off Bert's lap and licked his ankle. The sun slid underwater, leaving an arrow of red light in the place where it had last been.

After a moment, Bert said, "Y'okay?"

The young man, still kneeling, nodded unconvincingly as he wiped some of the grit off his face. He tried to speak but his lungs had not yet refilled and he could only wheeze.

"Take your time," Bert helpfully advised. "No shame staying down for the eight-count." He knew he should leave it at that, that he shouldn't get involved, that he was an old man and it was none of his business, but he couldn't resist saying, "What the hell was it about?"

The young man just shook his head so vigorously that it made his whole torso sort of waggle.

With curiosity cloaked in guilt, Bert said, "Well, whatever it was about, I kinda feel bad. Like maybe it was my fault. I mean, I kinda distracted ya."

"Wasn't your fault," the other managed. "Wasn't anything."

"Wasn't nothing. In fact it was pretty impressive and highly professional."

The young man shrugged. "They must've thought I was somebody else."

Bert just couldn't let that slide. "Come on, kid. You think I'm senile? You think I was born yesterday? You think I never seen a guy catch a beating before? What is it? Debts? Drugs? A woman?"

The young man didn't answer right away. He struggled to his feet, wincing a bit and gingerly touching his ribs. When he responded, it wasn't to Bert's words but to his accent and the breathy gruffness of his pauses. He said, "You from New York?"

"Yeah. And so are you, I'm guessing. Me, I'm from Brooklyn. Ass end'a President Street. Where we learned early on to recognize a coupla goombahs when we seen 'em."

The young man met Bert's gaze for just an instant, then retreated. "Must've thought I was someone else," he said again.

"Will you please stop insultin' my intelligence and come offa that? Lamest dodge inna book."

"Except in my case," the young man insisted, "it happens to be true. Sort of true, at least."

"Yeah, yeah."

"Because the person they probably thought I was is my twin brother. Identical. Same face."

As he said this he pointed vaguely toward himself as if offering his looks for inspection. And in fact his face was quite distinctive, sort of diamond-shaped. The top of his head was narrow, topped with a brush-cut mat of thick black hair. But the sides of his forehead angled outward toward cheekbones that were very wide; the sockets that held the restless dark eyes were unusually far apart. The jawline then tapered steeply inward toward a handsome square chin with a cleft so precise as to suggest a tap of a jeweler's chisel.

Bert stared at the face a moment then said, "Twin brother. Hm. I guess you could say that's a new wrinkle or a complicating factor which I had not previously considered. So your brother, he's in business with these goombahs?"

"No. Not exactly. Maybe sort of, you could say. But no, not really."

"That clears it up," said Bert. "What about you? You connected?"

The young man gave an uneasy laugh. "Me? No way."

Bert mulled a moment, gazing off at clouds that were changing from the candy pink of sunset to the brick red of early dusk. "Twin brother. Hm. But your mistaken identity story, it still doesn't quite wash."

The young man said nothing to that, just kicked absently at the cooling sand, sending a plume of it upward in a low arc. The chihuahua took this to be some kind of game and began pivoting and charging, jumping back and bobbing.

"And you know why it doesn't wash?" Bert went on. "It doesn't wash because there are beatings and there are beatings. If those goombahs really thought you were the guy they were mad at, you wouldn't have got off so easy. I mean, look at you. You can walk. You got teeth. What this says to me is that this wasn't a vendetta but a message. That make any sense to you?"

"Look, I don't really want to talk about it."

"Okay," said Bert with a shrug. "I get it. You'd rather just maintain a manly silence and slink away to lick your wounds in private like an injured lion or some other justly famous emblem of dignity and courage from the animal kingdom. I seen that on TV once. Injured lion alone under a bush. Very moving. Christ, that lion looked noble. And lonely. Well, okay, fine."

With difficulty the old man started to rise up from his folding chair, the fabric of his shirt rasping against the rough webbing. But as he slowly straightened up, he kept an eye on the young man's diamond-shaped face and on the forlorn expression he'd finally stopped trying to hide. Gathering up his chihuahua, he casually went on. "Or then again, on the other hand, you got a shirt and shoes and somethin' to put on over that banana hammock?"

The young man pointed with his chin toward the road that flanked the beach. "Yeah, stuff's in the car. Got a crappy little renter."

"So here's another idea," the old man said. "You've had a tough afternoon. What say I buy you a drink?"

2.

In fifteen years of living in Key West, Pete Amsterdam had never heard, seen, or read a single good thing about any of the City or County agencies. Most of the populace seemed to agree that the people who ran them were just plain stupid. A cynical minority disbelieved this and took the position that they were really quite clever but irredeemably corrupt. All seemed to agree that they were utterly ineffectual and perversely proud of it to boot, strangely smug about jobs not done, responsibilities shirked. Mayors and Councilmen came and went, but the gang of bubbas who actually ran things never seemed to change, though they did regularly swap jobs. One year's Building Inspector was next year's head of Sewers or chief of Road Maintenance; the Parking Authority was re-gifted like a Christmas fruitcake from cousin to cousin. Key Westers tended to shrug at the epic ineffectiveness of their local government, as they shrugged at nearly everything. What could they do about it? Besides, there was a certain subtropical charm in the languid bungling, a measure of comedic value in the ineptitude...until you needed something done.

Which Pete Amsterdam now did, badly. April was not ordinarily a buggy month, but something had gone very wrong this year and he was already being eaten alive by mosquitoes. In broad daylight, no less. Mosquitoes were flying in shimmering low formations above his little swimming pool. Spiraling swarms of them rode the thermals above his hot tub. Mosquitoes somehow squeezed through screens and tiny gaps in louvered windows to invade the house. They loitered on window sills and toilet seats and kitchen counters. And this at a time when the headlines were screaming about the Zika virus and dengue fever and West Nile.

Finally, in itchy desperation, expecting nothing but surly answers and excuses and frustration, he broke down and called the Monroe County Mosquito Control Board.

To his surprise, a dispatcher picked up on the third ring and sounded both sober and sympathetic as Amsterdam described his problem. "Hm," she said, "sounds serious. We'll have to send over a man and a PFU."

Impressed, Amsterdam said, "PFU?"

"Portable Fogging Unit," the dispatcher explained. "Best thing in these situations."

"Great," said Amsterdam. In spite of everything he knew about the bubba system, he felt a *frisson* of hope and the beginnings of gratitude. But this was still South Florida and he was waiting for the shakedown. "And this service, what's it cost?"

"Cost?" said the dispatcher. "There's no cost. It's why we're here. It's what we do."

At that Amsterdam felt vaguely ashamed. Here these nice people were willing to send over a PFU at no charge, and he'd been so ready to assume the worst about them. Why? Was he just one more snooty Yankee with a condescending attitude toward the local folks, the Conchs? Chastened, he said, "Well, I appreciate it. When do you think he might get here?"

"Busy day. Hopefully within the hour."

That had been four hours earlier; plenty of time to start thinking the worst again about the bubba system.

Waiting around, doing nothing but swatting mosquitoes and scouting for holes in screens, Amsterdam had stewed as his cherished afternoon rituals went unfulfilled: No tennis game at Bayview Park; no sunset viewed from White Street Pier. At last, just as dusk was settling in, a County pickup pulled up in front of the house.

"You the guy that called?" asked the man who emerged from the truck and clomped up the porch steps to the door. He was a tallish man, not fat, but with a sort of engulfing largeness about him. He made wide gestures, his elbows stuck out; you would not have wanted to sit next to him on a plane. He wore olive-green coveralls with a sweat-stain down the spine and embroidery on the right chest pocket that said *Ralphie.*

"Yeah, I called," said Amsterdam. "Half a day ago."

Unapologetically, Ralphie said, "Lotta houses. Lotta bugs. My opinion, gonna be a stinking bastard of a year for bugs. Where's the problem?"

"Everywhere. Mainly in the back."

He led Ralphie through the house and switched on a poolside floodlight. A miasma of mosquitoes instantly appeared in the beam. Ralphie cast an expert eye around the compact yard with its low palms and skyflower bushes and single scabby papaya tree that never fruited. Casually wiping a platoon of insects off of his uniform and forehead, he said, "Yeah, you got a problem here."

"So glad we agree," said Amsterdam.

"I'd say you got a Grade 2 infestation."

"Grade 2? What's grade 3, malaria?"

Impervious to sarcasm, Ralphie just stood there.

Amsterdam said, "So, um, what about the PFU?"

"First I have to finish the inspection."

He took out a flashlight and shined it around the property for fifteen seconds. Then he ticked an entry on the clipboard he was carrying. At that point, he put the clipboard down, reached into a deep pocket of his coveralls, and came out with a can of Raid. Motioning for Amsterdam to stand back, he gave it a shake and pressed the nozzle down so it hissed and issued forth a thin bluish haze of poison. He slowly pirouetted twice, a feeble and quickly disappearing trail of insecticide spiraling around him as he turned. Then he put the can back in his pocket.

Amsterdam said, "But what about the PFU?"

"That is the PFU," said Ralphie as he retrieved the clipboard and handed it to Amsterdam. "Could you please sign here that you received the service?"

"Service? What service did I receive? A fucking can of Raid from the hardware store?"

Serenely, Ralphie said, "That and the inspection."

Disgustedly, Amsterdam took the clipboard and grudgingly signed his name.

Ralphie tore off a copy of the form and handed it to him. Then he briefly looked down at his own copy. That's when everything changed.

"Hey, wait a second," he said. "Amsterdam. Pete Amsterdam.

You're the detective, right?"

"Wrong."

"Come on, sure you are. I remember that name. You're the guy that solved that big case a few years back."

"I never solved a case."

"Yeah, you did. You're just being modest. That big blackmail case with the two bad cops and Lefty Ortega's daughter."

"I didn't solve it. It solved itself. I happened to be standing there when it happened."

"Standing there with a gun in your hand," Ralphie said admiringly.

"Actually, it wasn't a gun. It was the TV remote. I grabbed it by mistake."

The mosquito man let that slide. "Boy, to solve that case. You must be a helluva detective. It's really lucky I came out here today."

"Lucky for you maybe," said Amsterdam, scratching a fresh bite on his wrist.

"I've sort of been thinking that maybe I should hire a detective," Ralphie said, almost shyly now.

"Yeah, I kind of picked up that's where you were going. But I'm not a detective, okay? Never really was. Don't even have a license anymore."

"License?" Ralphie asked. "Why didn't you say you had a problem with a license? City or County? I'll get you one by tomorrow."

"It's State. But I don't want a license, thank you."

"State, that would probably take a little longer."

"Listen, you don't seem to—"

"Mr. Amsterdam—"

"Pete."

"Pete, please, I'm serious. I got a problem."

"Who doesn't?"

"I'm not asking for myself. If it was for myself I'd shut up and go away. It's about this niece of mine—"

Amsterdam raised a hand. Mosquitoes buzzed around it, waiting for a chance to land and bite. "Stop," he said. "Please. Don't tell me. I don't want to hear about your problem. I don't want to hear about your niece, about how she's your favorite—"

"Well, she is my favorite. How'd you know?"

"Because that's always how it is. She's your favorite, she's a swell kid--"

"Well, she is. But she's, okay, a little odd, and—"

A bug bit Amsterdam just above his left eyebrow. It was one bite too many and he finally snapped.

"Listen, Ralphie. You have a problem. Your niece has a problem. Well, I have a problem too. My problem is that I'm living in a pestilential bog and you're on the public payroll and you show up four hours late and you don't do shit about it. So why should I give a fuck about your problem when it's obvious that you don't give a fuck about mine?"

Ralphie took this in with perfect calm and not a shred of umbrage. He spent a moment seeming to weigh the merits of the argument. Finally he said, "You know what, you're right. What I've done here, it's pretty half-ass. But since you're gonna help my niece—"

"Now wait a second—"

"I mean, what's fair is fair. You're gonna help my niece, which I really appreciate, I'm gonna make sure you get first-class treatment."

"Listen, Ralphie, I never said—"

"Gimme half an hour. I'll be back. And it'll be sayonara to the mosquitoes."

3.

U p in Naples—not the real, grimy, seedy Italian one, but the contrived and manicured rich folks' enclave on the west coast of Florida—a valet parker with a diamond-shaped face and a teal-colored polo shirt that said *Gregory* finally got the car he'd been waiting for.

During his few evenings' worth of shifts in the lot that backed the glitzy shops and overpriced restaurants of Third Street South, "Gregory" had been briefly behind the wheel of Porsches and Maseratis, Jags and Benzes and Aston-Martins and even the occasional Lamborghini. They were all nice automobiles, handsome rolling sculptures with sexily caressing seats and futuristic dashboards that glowed in restful shades of blue or green, and you could get them going pretty fast in the hundred yards or so between where you took possession of the vehicle and where you parked it. But life is choices, and the valet realized that at the pivotal moment he would have to settle on one single car.

So he gave it plenty of thought, because the car he drove would be crucial to the first impression he made; and that first impression, in turn, would become the keystone of the many details that added up to a consistent and therefore credible identity. Accordingly, he'd come around to the firm conclusion that the car he needed was a Bentley Continental GT W-12

Convertible. Everything about the car was perfect for his purpose. It was as stately as a Rolls, sitting high on enormous tires above the common run of sedans and coupes, suggesting solidity and all things respectable; but at the same time, it was sporty, rakish, debonair, especially in metallic blue with a subtly contrasting fabric top. The car's list-price was $262,775 and this alone would suggest a fair bit about the sort of man who'd drive one. Black sheep of a fabulously wealthy clan? Venture capitalist who'd cashed out? Brilliant but secretive entrepreneur? People would make assumptions. People always did. The assumptions made "Gregory's" job so much easier. All he had to do was play along with what people had already decided to believe.

It was getting close to 8 o'clock, by which time the Port Royal crowd had finished their at-home martinis and were starting to assemble for their sixty-dollar steaks, when his dream car came pulling up to the valet stand. The driver was a silver-haired gent with a silk sweater casually tied across his shoulders and a much younger wife who looked like she'd already had a fair amount of knife-work done. The valet opened their doors for them and, with due subservience, wished them a nice evening. Then he slid into the butt-warm driver's seat, drove to the south exit of the lot, turned west on Thirteenth Avenue, north on Gulfshore Boulevard, and just kept going.

He was on his way to pick up a young woman who thought his name was Justin Prendergast-Snead and who believed that he was very rich.

4.

"But I haven't introduced myself," said the young man who'd been pummeled at the beach, offering a hand. "Ned Preston."

They were sitting at a place called the Eclipse Saloon, a semi-dive in an unfashionable location, Bert's favorite watering hole for many years now. Tourists seldom found the place. It wasn't on Duval Street and it wasn't on the water and it wasn't open-air. It was snug and dim, like Bert thought a tavern should be, with a padded bar that you could rest your elbows on and a smoky mirror that sweetly reflected the elegant shapes of the booze bottles.

"Preston, eh? Kind of white bread. I took you for Italian."

"Well, I am. I mean, I was. I mean I guess I still am, sort of."

"Sort of?" said Bert. "In my book, you're Italian or you're not. It's not something you get over, like a head cold."

"Right, right," said Ned. "What I mean is, I'm still Italian but my father changed the family name."

The old man couldn't quite stifle a frown at that. For all his experience, there were still things about the world that he didn't quite get, and one of them was this impulse to change rich and colorful family names to bland, generic ones. Shapiro becoming Shepard, Righetti dulling out to Riggs, Morales morphing into Martin. This rush to assimilation; he considered it a form of surrender. Whatever happened to family pride, to honoring those who'd gone before, to remembering where you came from? Somewhat sourly, Bert said, "He become Episcopalian too?"

Just slightly defensively, Ned said, "Look, he changed the name right after his old man went off to the slammer, okay?"

"Ah," said Bert. "Guess that changes things a little bit. A whaddyacallit, a blot on the family reputation. So what was the name before?"

"You wouldn't know it. My grandfather was just a small-time guy."

"Try me."

Softly, seeming somewhat pained but resigned, the young man said, "Pestucci. My grand-dad was Nunzio Pestucci."

Trying to place the name, Bert reached down to his lap and rubbed his dog's head. He did this to help him think, like he was rubbing his own chin. No dogs were allowed at the Eclipse, but Bert always brought his in anyway. For form's sake, he'd try to hide the dog in a fold of an alpaca cardigan or a velour V-neck, but the dog's nose or ears would be sticking out and everybody knew it was there and no one cared.

Finally the old man said, "Nunzio Pestucci. Yeah, I remember him. Mostly ran juke boxes and cigarette machines and pinball down in Bay Ridge. Strong-armed 'em into candy stores, bowling alleys, shit like that. I think they finally got him on a RICO charge. Offered him immunity to testify but he wouldn't sing."

At the mention of this last word, something inconvenient happened. The chihuahua in Bert's lap craned its scrawny neck and began to howl. The howl was a three-note aria and the notes never varied. Ow-ow-OWWW! Ow-ow-OWWW!

Heads turned at the bar. To the dog, Bert said, "Not now, Nacho." Gently but firmly, as if re-loading a jack-in-the-box, he shoved the tiny creature back down into the folds of his cabana jacket. To Ned, he said, "Sorry. Brilliant dog knows exactly one trick but he has no idea when he should do it. So anyway, you were saying?"

Ned sipped some beer then vigorously wiped his lips like he was trying to erase that part of the family saga. "Um, about my grandfather going off to jail. My father was just finishing law school when it happened."

"Not a great start to a legal career," Bert conceded.

"My brother and I were ten."

"Your brother, right. So about this mysterious—"

Thinking aloud, Ned said, "I sort of think that was the beginning of all his problems."

"Your grandfather going off to jail?"

"No, my father changing everybody's name. I think it really messed my brother up. Messed with his whole sense of who he was."

Bert considered that, sipped his Manhattan, and glanced around the comfortingly familiar saloon. The ancient mounted trophy fish were badly in need of dusting.

After a moment, Ned went on. "I mean, there's a lot of stuff that goes with names, right? So like, one day he's Richie Pestucci, neighborhood kid, funny, lighthearted, bit of a goofball. Then all of a sudden he's Richard Preston. That sounds totally opposite, doesn't it? Serious, formal, like you should call him mister. But who the hell is that guy? I think the sudden change really confused my brother. So one thing led to another and naturally he became a professional impostor and a con man and a criminal and a fraud."

At that Bert put his glass down and raised a wrinkled and yellowish hand. "Whoa, hold on a second. I thought I was paying pretty good attention but that last segue kind of snuck up on me. Your father changed his name, so naturally your brother became a con man?"

Ned traced a finger around the damp edge of his beer glass. "Look, who can say why anyone becomes anything? But yeah, I think that's how it started. He didn't know who he was, so he decided he could play at being anybody. Started innocently enough. I think it started with nicknames."

"Nicknames?" said Bert. "What's the harm with nicknames? I knew lotsa guys with nicknames. Vinnie Fish. Frankie Bread. Didn't mean they were con men or schizo or anything like that."

"Yeah, but did they name themselves? I mean, kids *get* nicknames, right? Not my brother. He picked his own. *Flash. Knuckles. Big Cat.* He'd have a new one every month or so. Then he started messing around with disguises. You know, kid stuff, fake eyeglasses, rubber noses, dime-store wigs, that type of thing. For a while it was cute."

"Musta been a laugh a minute around the Pestucci dinner table," Bert put in.

"The Preston dinner table," Ned corrected. "And yeah, some of it was funny. But there was something off about it, something dark. By high school it was getting pretty mean, like he wanted to show people how easy it was to fool them, turn 'em into suckers."

"Not a good way to make friends," said Bert.

"He didn't have friends. He had marks. I'll give you an example. First day at a new school, he gets hold of a wheelchair, pretends he can't walk. Says he forgot his lunch money. Gets kids to roll him around, pay for his lunch and also for his cab fare home. He got beat up for it next day, but you know what? He didn't care. He'd won his little game. He'd outsmarted people. He seemed to get off on that. Plus I think it was the first time he'd scammed people out of money. Got to be a very bad habit."

Bert nipped at his cocktail and said, "No offense, but he sounds like quite a piece of work, your brother."

Ned just shook his diamond-shaped head. "Man, you don't know the half of it. You don't know a tenth of it. I could tell you stories—"

"I got time," said Bert. "Want a burger?"

At the mention of the word, the chihuahua in the old man's lap started doing a stiff-legged dance all over his crotch while staring up imploringly with glassy black eyes that captured an improbable amount of light in the dim tavern.

"Nah, thanks," said Ned Preston. "My ribs still hurt too much."

"Well, I'm gonna have a burger," said Bert. "Dog starts getting hungry this time of the evening."

5.

When Ralphie from Mosquito Control returned to Pete Amsterdam's house, he wasn't driving a pickup truck, but rather a more substantial vehicle carrying a big tank that was painted orange and shaped like an enormous *mortadella*. On the back and sides of the tank there were stencils of a skull and crossbones. Noting the icon, Amsterdam said, "Poison?"

"And you say you're not a detective," Ralphie answered.

"What I mean is, is it toxic?"

"Of course it's toxic. What do you think I'm spraying, Right Guard? Chanel Number 5?"

"To humans, I mean. Or pets," said Amsterdam, who was wrestling with the classic liberal dilemma of wanting to murder things he didn't like but to do it kindly.

"Toxic to everything," Ralphie said cheerily. "There a cat around? I'll demonstrate. Hey, just kidding. Look, it's a short-acting poison. Close the house up for ten, fifteen minutes and you're fine. Here's your gas mask."

"Gas mask?"

"Better safe than sorry. You don't have asthma, emphysema, lung cancer, anything like that?"

"Not so far," said Amsterdam, as he struggled to get the mask over his nose and mouth and to snug up the straps behind his head. When he had it more or less in place, he tried to ask Ralphie if he had it on right but his voice came out sounding like a kazoo.

Ralphie gave him a thumbs-up and started unwinding a thick orange hose from a reel beneath the tank.

"Lemme close the windows!" Amsterdam buzzed.

Ralphie dragged the hose through the side yard, positioned it strategically near the swimming pool, and opened the gas cock. A hellish yellow haze spewed forth from the nozzle. Looking almost liquidy at first, it spread in all directions into a billowing scalloped cloud, a noxious fog that rose briefly skyward then dimmed and settled back like an extinguished Roman candle. Within thirty seconds dead frogs were dropping out of trees like overripe fruit, landing on the pool apron with faint moist splats. Huge palmetto bugs rolled onto their backs like exhausted hookers and feebly waved their useless legs in the air. An unlucky crow that had been flying past went into an abrupt and shallow kamikaze dive and brained itself against a palm tree. Turning off the poison and buzzing through his mask, Ralphie said, "Well, that should do it. Now let's talk about my niece."

When they had settled into old-Florida-style wicker chairs in the mosquito-free living room, Amsterdam said, "I'll hear you out because a deal's a deal, but I'm telling you there is like zero chance I'll be able to help."

Rather than addressing that directly, Ralphie fingered the wide arm of his chair and looked around the house. "Nice place," he said. Pointing toward a newer addition that angled off the entryway, he said, "What's over there?"

"My wine room and my music room."

"Ah, I thought maybe it was your detective office."

"That's what the IRS thought, too. But you wanted to talk to me about your niece—"

"You're getting curious now, aren't you?"

"No, I'm not," said Amsterdam, but the annoying truth was that he was. He tried his damnedest to squelch the dangerous impulse.

"Thought you might get curious," Ralphie said, "if I, like, skirted the subject a little bit. That's something you ought to know about us Conchs, Pete. We usually don't go right at things. We consider that, oh, I don't know, a little pushy, a little rude. A little northern. No offense. We sort of like to ease in, circle around."

"And I'd sort of like to finish up and get some dinner."

Ralphie ignored that. "Another thing about us," he went on, "we hardly ever leave the Keys. I mean, maybe for vacation now and then, we'll hop over to New Orleans, take a cruise, stuff like that. But we almost never move away. Why would we? Here, we got family, we got friends, we got jobs, we got property. Why would we leave?"

"Um, maybe to see a little more of the world? Beyond this little chain of rocks and dive motels, I mean."

"This is what I'm getting to," said Ralphie. "My niece, Renita her name is, that's the way she sees it. Always has. Had this travel bug from the time she was a little kid. Wanted to go away to school. Wanted to see Paris, go to Rome, learn Chinese, whatever. Anything, kind of, that would get her out of here. Rest of the family thought she was a little weird."

"But you said she's your favorite," Amsterdam put in.

"Of course she is. I said she's weird, I didn't say I didn't like her. Weird is fine with me. That sense of adventure, that restlessness. I don't get it but I admire it."

"So did she get to Paris?"

"She got to Tallahassee," Ralphie said. "Got accepted to State. That was, what, three years ago. I think that's really when the trouble started."

"Three years ago? Can we skip to a little closer to now?"

"Hey, I'm trying to paint you a picture here."

"Fine, but it doesn't have to be the Sistine Chapel."

Undiscouraged, Ralphie said, "So she went off to Tallahassee. Decided to major in Psychology. I wish she'd picked something else. Marketing. Nursing."

"Something more practical?" said Amsterdam.

"Nah, something less...less morbid."

"Psychology is morbid?"

"Sure sounds that way to me. Look, Renita and me, we talk on the phone a lot. I ask her what she's studying. Phobias. Anxiety. Depression. Paranoia. Addicted lab rats. Steady diet of that just can't be good for a person."

The detective said, "But lots of kids study—"

Ralphie talked over him, but very softly, almost as if he half hoped he would not be heard. His eyes slid away like he was telling a secret he shouldn't tell but that would gnaw his guts out if he didn't. "And the thing is," he said, "I'm not a hundred percent sure my niece is all that stable to begin with."

It was the tone more than the words that stopped Amsterdam cold. Ralphie was a big gruff man who worked with poison and killed things for a living. Suddenly he didn't sound big and gruff. He sounded tender and he sounded scared.

"Listen, Pete," he went on, "us Conchs, we don't talk bad about family. Not to outsiders. Not ever. I'm trusting you here, okay?"

Amsterdam stifled a secret shudder. Being trusted carried with it a responsibility, and responsibility was exactly what he didn't want, what he'd moved to Key West to avoid. His lips moved with an impulse to protest, to fend. All he managed to say was, "Want a beer or something?"

Ralphie said he'd love one. Pete went to the fridge.

"So the thing about Renita," her uncle went on after the first suck of his drink, "is that she just hasn't had an easy time of it. Right from the start. Shitty parents. Christ forgive me for saying it, but it's true. My brother Clyde, I love him, but he drinks too much, he yells, he's scary sometimes. His wife, Carina, she should never have been a mom. She was a bit of a slut before she got married and I think the only thing that's really changed is that guys don't chase after her any more. She cares about her fucking fingernails more than she cares about her daughter.

"So the kid didn't get enough attention growing up. Only child. Spent a lot of time alone. Painted pictures. Wrote down stories. Stuff was a little spooky sometimes."

"Spooky?" said Amsterdam.

"Hard to remember details," Renita's uncle said. "More just a feeling I'd get. Like if there was a picture of a girl in a room, it would feel like she was locked inside. Or she'd draw a rabbit, the rabbit looked sad and maybe some of its fur or one of its ears was missing. Just stuff like that. Anyway, then in high school she never seemed to have many friends. Not until all that social media stuff got started. Then she had lots. Rich friends, artist friends, friends all over the world. She'd tell me about them. Only problem was she never actually met any of them. Basically sat in her room fantasizing about how great it would be if she did."

He paused for a long pull of his beer. It wasn't until he paused that he seemed to notice how much he'd been talking. Suddenly a little sheepish, he said, "Jeez, Pete, I don't mean to go rambling on—"

"It's okay, Ralphie. Talk to me."

The big man chewed his lip and nodded. "Okay. Okay. So she goes away to college. I'm thinking, great, she's away from her parents, away from Key West, she'll start getting out more, have more of, like, a regular life. But just the opposite happens. She just doesn't click with the kids at school. I don't know why. Maybe real flesh and blood people just couldn't measure up to her make-believe friends on the computer. She gets even more isolated. I talk on the phone with her almost every day. Some days I think I'm the only person she's talked with all day long. She sounds pretty spacey some of the time. Plus they keep throwing all this crazy stuff at her in her classes. Obsessions. Compulsions. Complexes. Syndromes. She tells me about them and I get this weird feeling that she's not just doing schoolwork, she's trying to figure out how many of 'em she has."

At that Amsterdam finally broke in. "Ralphie, listen, you're concerned about your niece. I sympathize. I really do. But I don't see any reason that you need a detective. A therapist, maybe. A counselor."

Ralphie shook his head and raised a hand. "But wait, Pete, this is what I'm getting to. A few days ago I'm talking to her and she tells me she's writing a paper about this thing called the Stockholm Syndrome. Ever hear of it?"

"Sounds familiar," Amsterdam said. "Is that the one where the hostages—"

"That's right," said Ralphie. "Hostages, captives. They come around to liking or even loving the guys that capture them. So Renita's telling me about this, and I find myself getting pretty upset."

"Upset? Why upset?"

Ralphie fidgeted as he struggled to find words. "Upset because it's *wrong*. I mean, capturing people, holding them. It's wrong." He broke off, sipped some beer, then with a great effort brought himself to look the detective squarely in the eye. "Nah, that's not why I got upset. I got upset because Renita was defending the whole thing, like she found it appealing, sexy even, like it all made perfect sense to her. That scared me. It sounded, I hate to say it, a little nutty."

"It's just a school paper," Amsterdam put in.

"That's exactly what she said," Renita's uncle replied. "But then, like five seconds later, she tells me about this date she has coming up. She's all wound up about it. It's in Naples. Guy's sending a private plane to pick her up. Guy she met online, of course. Guy who lives a completely different kind of life."

"What else she tell you about him?"

"In that conversation, nothing," Ralphie said. "But we talked again that evening. Then she gushed a while. Guy's name is Justin. Thirty years old. Successful business guy. Artsy. Well-traveled. Rich family with a mansion on the Gulf."

"And yet," mused Amsterdam, "he's dredging the internet for undergraduate Psych majors. That didn't strike your niece as strange?"

"Apparently not. Look, she's lonely. She's got big daydreams. To her he sounded pretty fabulous."

"Peachy," said the unwilling detective. "So what's the problem?"

"Well, she makes her plans, she's all excited, and then at the last minute things don't work out with the private plane."

"Ah. Imagine that."

"Guy tells her it turns out his father's using the plane," Ralphie said. "Says he's had his travel person check all over for commercial flights. Everything's booked solid. He's so disappointed. It would have been so great to get together, but he guesses it'll have to wait. Unless by any chance she feels like driving down. This sound fishy to you, Pete?"

"Like last week's chowder."

"Well, my niece decides maybe she'll drive. It's only eight, nine hours. She asks me what I think of the idea. I kind of walk on eggs with Renita. I never like to criticize. So I just say be careful, there's a lot of creeps out there. And she says—"

"Wait," Amsterdam cut in. "Let me guess. She says don't worry, she trusts her gut, she's got good instincts."

"Yeah, that's pretty much what she said. How'd you know?"

"Because that's what young people always say when they really have no idea what they're doing. So then what happened?"

Ralphie reached up and rubbed his neck as though he had a sudden spasm in it. "I don't know. That's the last I spoke with her."

"And when was that?"

"This morning."

"This morning?" blurted Amsterdam, and he couldn't quite hold back something close to a laugh. "That's like no time at all. That's way too soon to start worrying."

"It's unusual, is all," the uncle said, trying to sound calm but squeezing the arms of his chair. "Three, four times I've called her and she hasn't called me back. That never happens. Look, call me nuts, but I got a bad feeling about this whole thing."

"Ralphie, your niece is a woman of legal age who's out on a date. Due respect, maybe it's not the first thing on her mind to take a call from you."

The big man looked down at his lap and his helpless expression made Amsterdam feel bad for being flip.

Softening his tone, he went on, "Look, you want my opinion? She's having an adventure and I hope she's enjoying the heck out of it. Odds are she'll be disappointed in the end, but so what? Isn't that how most dates turn out? You don't get a detective involved every time a loved one has a disappointing date."

"Yeah, I guess you're right," Renita's uncle said. "No real reason to worry." He didn't sound the slightest bit persuaded.

The unsettling truth was that Amsterdam wasn't totally persuaded either. In spite of himself, he'd begun to catch the contagion of concern about the mosquito man's peculiar niece. Without realizing he was about to do so, he reached across the small space that separated them and gave his visitor a reassuring pat on the shoulder. "Listen, Ralphie, I can't tell you not to worry. But I can tell you not to panic. I'll bet you hear from her very soon. If you do, if you don't, either way you'll let me know, okay?"

6.

At the Eclipse Saloon, Bert the Shirt was almost finished with his burger. Actually, he'd given most of it, the meat part at least, to the ecstatic, snorting little dog who was still prancing around in his lap. Bert marveled at how much meat the dog could eat. Dog weighed, what, three, four pounds? If a man ate like that in proportion to his weight, he'd need a steak the size of a manhole cover. And it would clog him up but good. Whereas the dog's digestion was amazing. Nothing threw it off. The dog would eat, go outside, leave a pile. Every time. Then again, the dog was young. Bert envied the dog's youth but did not begrudge it. In fact he celebrated it as he fed the insatiable chihuahua yet another crumbly morsel of rare chopped beef. The dog licked greedily but gently at the old man's oily fingers, and it very dimly occurred to Bert that this was probably about as close as a man could get to suckling a baby.

At Bert's elbow, Ned Preston was saying, "...And that's the scam that really set the pattern, that really shows the way my brother operates."

Bert said, "Huh?"

The young man with the diamond-shaped face looked at him a moment, appearing rather puzzled.

Bert was embarrassed, but not very. He'd learned by now to cut himself some slack on occasions when he'd lost the thread of a conversation or just given himself a brief timeout from the hard work of listening. "Sorry," he said. "Got distracted by the stupid dog. Mind rewinding it a little bit?"

Ned gave a small shrug and nipped at the beer he'd been nursing. "Sure," he said. "So, it was his first big con-job, the one where he called himself Jeremiah Effingham-Schwartz. Gets caught stealing passports in a youth hostel in Boston, but he manages to hide one in his underwear. Takes it on the lam to Toronto, where he wears a Wounded Warrior cap and dog tags and claims he's a four-tour Afghanistan vet fleeing anti-Semitic harassment in the U.S. Army. What pacifist Canadian Jew wouldn't buy it? So some nice idealistic support-group guy takes him into his home, starts working on a political asylum case. My brother lifts his credit cards and birth certificate, steals his car, and drives it all the way to Las Vegas, where there's a big convention going on for pharmaceutical salesmen. He convinces the desk clerk he's a rep for Pfizer named August DeFiore-O'Malley and gets a room charged to the company. At some convention party he picks up a woman and tells her he's really Angus Jocko McCallan, a DJ from Scotland. She's charmed by his brogue, and off they go to LA together, where he gloms a platinum Amex card from a restaurant table, goes to Beverly Hills and gets his teeth capped for $46,000. Eventually, he's busted when the stolen car gets picked up for a traffic violation and he goes off to prison for a couple years."

Bert, now once again listening intently, said, "Prison? So he isn't too damn clever after all."

"Actually, he is," Ned Preston disagreed. "Going to jail is like a sabbatical for him. Lets him recharge, relax, plan next moves. You know what he does in prison? He reads obituaries, looking for people who don't need their identities anymore. He practices different accents, polishes routines. Plus he's the model prisoner, his sentences always get shortened after meetings with the warden and some chaplain. I mean, what's easier to fake than having seen the light, found Jesus, gotten on a better path?"

Bert said, "Yeah, but how many times can you pull that dodge?"

"So far? Two. First time he got out, he went straight to a nice suburban neighborhood and started rifling mailboxes. Found a check from a local ad agency, mastered the signature and had some new ones printed up, put a deposit on a BMW and drove to Boise, Idaho, where he became Jean-Pierre Sabatier-Windsor, a Cambridge-trained thespian with a calling to class up the local theater troupe. Within six months, he'd had sex with Lady Macbeth, Eliza Doolittle, and Blanche DuBois, plus grabbed a trove of Visa card imprints complete with expiration dates. Blew town, went to Bend, Oregon where he pretended to be a Stanford prof named Alonzo Gittlestein-Puig who'd lost his job because of some conniving between Microsoft and the CIA, but who meanwhile had a child who was dying of cancer and dreamed of seeing the Great Wall of China. The repo man finally caught up with him in Walla Walla, Washington, took the Beamer and turned him in."

"Doesn't have good luck with cars," Bert observed.

"Guess not," said Ned. "Or maybe he just needed another vacation. So back in jail, he starts working on a whole different—"

The young man suddenly fell silent because Bert had raised his hand, a crinkly index finger pointing straight up toward the low ceiling of the tavern. "Excuse me," he said, "but may I please interject one thing at this particular moment? This account, fascinating though it is, is it gonna, like, at any point in time connect or let's say intersect with the more recent event of you getting beat up onna beach by a coupla goombahs who you claim, rather unconvincingly I might add, might have mistaken you for your brother?"

Ned Preston seemed surprised and perhaps just slightly miffed at the question. "Will it connect? Of course it'll connect. It's just that it's, you know, a little complicated."

"Ain't it always," said Bert the Shirt, and gestured for another round of drinks.

7.

At that moment, in Naples, Renita Daughtry was pulling in under the gracious *porte cochere* of the Gulf's Edge Hotel.

The valet was deeply unimpressed with her car. It was a twelve-year old Nissan with a missing hubcap and crumbly rings of rust around the headlights and a sheet of plastic stretched and taped over what used to be the right rear window. The hotel, on the other hand, was quite spiffy and elegant, seven stories tall, ringed by royal palms, festooned with balconies, nestled into the narrow and precious swath of real estate between the Boulevard and the beach. The hotel just didn't get guests with cars like that. Its dishwashers had nicer cars than that.

The bellman wasn't too taken with the new arrival's cheap and mismatched luggage either.

Still, when Renita strolled into the lobby she gave no outward sign of feeling outclassed or overwhelmed. In fact, if you didn't look too closely, she seemed poised and confident beyond her years, and miles beyond her very limited experience of the wider world. Partly, this was simply because she was tall and pretty.

Her prettiness was not of the classic, even-featured kind; nor could it really be called glamorous. But when people caught a glimpse of her, they almost always looked again. She was quietly exotic, ambiguous, a jigsaw puzzle that somehow came together as a memorable picture. Like most Conchs, she had a wildly varied heredity, contributions coming from old New England ship captains and Cuban cigar-rollers and Bahamian fishermen and Creole ladies from New Orleans. The shaking of the genetic dice had given her bright green eyes and jet-black hair with a widow's peak that seemed made for a *mantilla*. She had the generous hips and slender calves of the Caribbean, yet her skin, even beneath the chronic suntan, was rather pale, with surprising faint suggestions of Irish freckles on the sides of her small straight nose. The lips were full, a shade darker than the eraser on a pencil, dimpled with light striations that would give texture to a kiss. Because she spent so much time alone and so relatively little in ordinary social situations, she'd developed an unconscious and disarming habit of holding people's gazes just a fraction of a second longer than they were used to, stretching moments of contact by some part of a beat.

But it wasn't just her looks and stature that allowed her to move with such apparent ease through the fancy hotel lobby. It was that, in her daydreams at least, she'd rehearsed this sort of thing. In her fantasies, she'd been in hotels like this many times before. She'd moved with grace past potted palms and intimate settees where people in silk clothing drank champagne from dainty flutes; she'd strolled without qualm or jitters toward registration desks made of fine mahogany.

She did so now as if she had finally, belatedly, stepped into the life she'd been meant all along to have. "Good evening," she said to the clerk, "Checking in, please." And she gave her name.

The clerk, although he didn't quite approve of the young woman's bright pink blouse with some sort of frou-frou on the collar and the placket, smiled with an attempt at warmth, glanced at his computer, and said, "Yes, of course. Welcome. Your room has been pre-paid by a Mr. Prendergast-Snead."

"That was lovely of him," said Renita, secretly laughing at herself for saying it. She vaguely knew that no one talked that way except in costume dramas set in England.

"And how many guests will be staying with us?" the clerk asked.

Was there something just very faintly salacious in the question? Renita could not be sure, though she supposed it would be understandable. Young woman in an unfamiliar town being put up in a waterfront hotel paid for by a fabulously wealthy and just slightly older man. People could think what they wanted. But in Renita's mind it was crystal clear that she had not come to Naples to jump into bed with Justin Prendergast-Snead. She'd been quite definite about that in her emails. She was not a prude but she didn't sleep with strangers. That just wasn't her, and he shouldn't take anything for granted. She'd stay at the hotel; he'd bivouac at the family manse. She wanted to meet him, talk, walk on the beach, maybe hold hands, see the sun go down together. After that, she'd follow her heart; she'd wait and see if she felt captivated. That's what she always did in her imaginings and it had worked out pretty well so far. "One guest, thank you."

"One guest. Fine," said the clerk. "Mr. Prendergast-Snead has left a message for you. He'll be here at 8:00 to pick you up. In the meantime, may I have a bellman show you to your room?"

8.

By the third beer, Ned Preston's cardboard coaster had become damp enough with condensation that he could rub off the top layer with a fingertip and roll the shreds of wet paper into little crescents. He found this quite relaxing. The paper crescents grew into a pile as he went on with his story.

"So those guys who beat me up," he finally admitted. "It's not that they mistook me for my brother. They already figured out I'm not. I've run into them before down here."

"Now we're bein' logical. Now we're gettin' somewhere."

"They just got tired of me getting in their way."

Bert lowered his voice just in case anyone else in the dim bar was trying to hear their conversation. No one was. The other patrons were talking about fishing or politics or thong bikinis. "Getting in their way for what? This is what I'm asking."

"I'm getting to it, I'm getting to it," said Ned as he drank some beer. "Okay, so the second time my brother's in prison, he starts working on a Russian accent. Russian accents are hard. Lots of phlegmy kind of sounds, lots of *kh* sounds that give you a sore throat. Try it."

Bert said, *"Kh. Kh."* Sure enough, it bothered his throat.

"Vowels like an adenoid infection," Ned went on. "But he gets it down. Also, he saves up every penny he makes from working in the prison laundry, because in his new role he's gonna need some cash to throw around. So he goes back into the world as Alexei Popov-Krichevski and he starts hanging around in a strip club out by LaGuardia. Wears nice suits, showy jewelry, drinks Cristal. Lets people think what they want to think anyway—that he's some Russian mob guy.

"But here's the masterstroke in his routine: He gives big tips to all the strippers even though he hardly looks at them. They're writhing around a pole, he sits there looking at his cuticles. They're hanging naked off trapezes, he's reading the *Post*. People notice. How can this guy be so blasé unless he can have these women whenever he wants, unless they're working for him or someone he controls?

"So he invests a couple weeks and a few grand in this persona," Ned Preston went on, "until he finds his mark. The mark is a little guy who comes in alone almost every evening between 5:30 and 7:00. Thinning hair, weak chin, you get the picture. Anyway, he's there a lot, and one evening my brother has a bottle of champagne sent over to his table. Then he goes over, very graciously, and says, 'I vant to thenk you for your business. You are good customer. I appreciate.'

"So the mark says, 'Oh, you're the owner?'

"My brother says, 'Better from owner. I am lendlord. Owner gets headaches. Lendlord gets money and ladies. Five thousand dollars every week. New ladies every month. Is good. I leave you now to enjoy the show.'

"So another week goes by. My brother's there every evening. Most evenings the mark comes in. They nod at each other. The mark feels good to be noticed by the bigshot landlord. Then one evening my brother walks over to his table. 'Pleess,' he asks. 'I can speak with you a minute?'

"The mark invites him to sit down. My brother says very calmly, 'Thenk you.' He pauses. He smiles. Without dropping the smile he says, 'Do not turn around, but behind you there are two men who khave just arrived from Moscow. Sent by Putin. Yes, by Putin khimself. I em proud to tell you I em enemy of Putin. But I em sed to tell you they are khere to kill me...No, pleess, do not turn around.'"

Ned broke off to sip some beer, and Bert the Shirt said, "Wait. So lemme guess what happens next. Just a wild guess. Your brother tells the guy he needs to get of town in a hurry and offers him the deed on the strip club at a fire-sale price."

"Bingo," the young man said.

Bert said, "Variation on the old or one might even say quaint or classic Brooklyn Bridge scenario. You're telling me people still fall for that?"

"I'm telling you people haven't gotten any smarter. Plus the guy wasn't really thinking about the money. He was thinking about the monthly shipment of strippers. Tends to cloud guys' judgment."

"So how much did your brother take him for?"

"Two hundred grand. Delivered in cash next night in the parking lot."

"Tidy," said Bert. He fished a whisky-soaked maraschino cherry from the bottom of his glass and fed it to the dog. The dog ate it stem and all. Almost at once it began to wobble in the old man's lap. "Except there's more to it than that or else you wouldn't'a gotten beat up onna beach."

"Yeah, there is," said Ned, in a rather downhearted murmur. "My genius brother fucked up a little bit. He should've done a little research about the guy he picked to con. Turns out the mark was a nephew of Funzi Albertini. That name mean anything to you?"

"Christ yeah, it does. The Butcher of Rego Park. People still call him that?"

"Yeah, they do. And it turns out this nephew of his, Marco, who came across as just a mild-mannered little creep, is all set up to inherit the title. When he's not gawking at T & A, the guy's a stone-cold killer with a crew of stone-cold killers."

"Jeez," said Bert, not without a certain measure of sympathy for the con man, "that's a bad break."

"Bad break or just plain stupid or a death wish. I mean, guy wants to run a strip club scam, fine. But there are strip clubs everywhere. Cleveland. Phoenix. Orlando. Why would he pick a strip club near LaGuardia? Why pick a neighborhood that probably has more wiseguys per square mile than anyplace this side of Palermo?"

The question didn't need answering and Bert didn't answer it. Ned's brother had been spitting in the eye of destiny. That much was clear. The old man just said, "Ya know, helping someone, saving someone, even a brother, there's only so much you can do."

Ned rolled some more wet paper from his coaster.

Bert adjusted his drunk dog then went on. "But wait a second. Here's what I don't see. How'd you get involved inna first place? How'd you end up inna middle?"

"Just lucky, I guess," the young man said with a mirthless laugh. "The scam I heard about from my brother. We were talking almost every day while this was going on. He knew I didn't approve but he also knew I couldn't talk him out of anything. As soon as he scored the money, he told me he was treating himself to a little vacation in Key West."

"Figures."

"What figures?"

"That he'd pick Key West," said Bert. "Guy's a world-class liar, faker, bullshit artist. Where's he gonna feel more at home? But okay, he heads to Key West. He's figured out by now that he accidentally ripped off the Mob?"

"No. He had no idea. I'm the one who found that out."

Bert couldn't help sounding instantly suspicious. "You? You said you wasn't connected."

"I'm not. I heard about it at my job. I pump cappuccino in Queens. Pays the rent. And here's something maybe you didn't know: Even wiseguys go to Starbucks these days. So I'm working my shift on Astoria Boulevard and I hear guys talking about how this guy Marco got scammed. Telling the story, guys are laughing. They're laughing less when they talk about what's gonna happen to the guy when Marco catches him. He's gonna die, of course. But slowly. And with the phony deed rammed up his ass."

The usually unflappable Bert winced a bit at that. It reminded him he was overdue for a colonoscopy. He sipped his drink and said, "So Marco and these goombahs head out to find your brother."

"Exactly."

"But how would they know where to look? How would they know he headed to Key West?"

Ned shook his head with a mixture of exasperation and wonderment. "My brother," he said. "It's not enough that he cons a guy, he's gotta really rub it in. So after taking this guy Marco's money, he also steals his car."

"Oy, again with the car stuff," said Bert the Shirt.

"What can I say? He likes to steal cars. But what he doesn't realize is that Marco's phone is in the glove box. So he drives all night and all next day, and then, just as he's getting to Key West in the evening, he hears the phone ring, and he jumps, and he figures, shit, someone could've been tracing the phone the whole time."

"Tracing the phone?" the old man said. "Like some high-tech Homeland Security thing?"

"Nah, anybody can do it. Tracer's built right into the phone."

"Right into the phone? Like, it finds itself? What a fucking world...But wait. He still doesn't know that it's a Mob guy's car, right?"

"No, no idea. What he's afraid of is that the cops are tracking him."

"Are they?"

With mounting exasperation, Ned said, "No. But Marco might be tracking him. But my brother has no way of knowing that. In any case, he realizes that maybe he's being traced and he freaks. He calls me up. By bad luck, I'm in spin class, music's blasting, I don't hear the phone. I get his message an hour later. Completely paranoid. He's pulled the phone out of the glove box and smashed it. He's ditching the car, stashing the money—"

"Wait a second," said Bert. "Stashing the money?"

"Yeah. Can't risk getting caught with two hundred grand in a briefcase. Says he's hiding it at some construction site. Then he tells me he's smashing his own phone too, turning off email, doesn't want anything that could leave a trail. He'll call me when he can."

Bert said, "So you never got to warn him about Marco?"

"No, I didn't. That's why I came down here to find him. What else could I do?"

"Fair enough," said Bert. "But if your brother was so freaked, so jumpy, what makes you think he even stayed in town? Maybe he took off somewhere."

Rather helplessly, Ned Preston said, "Maybe he did. I don't know. I don't know anything. Except my ribs hurt."

There was a silence then. Instant by instant it was filled by the lulling sounds of the mostly empty tavern. Beer hissed softly as it hit the bottom of a glass. A rumble of gruff laughter came from a far corner. Bert the Shirt was thinking about people like the Albertinis and the rules they played by, and he determined the con man's survival chances were very poor. "Maybe you should go home, Ned," the old man said at last. "You've already taken a beating for your brother. What more can you do?"

"Find him before they do. 'Cause if I don't, he dies. Say it was your brother, Bert. Wouldn't you do the exact same thing?"

9.

Richie Pestucci, aka Richard Preston, aka Justin Prendergast-Snead, aka a couple of dozen other things, had not dared to hang around Key West, of course, but had taken off for Naples for no other reason than that that's where the first Greyhound out of town was heading.

Now, having pulled an elegantly understated cotton crew-neck sweater over his monogrammed valet parker's shirt, he was driving someone else's Bentley at a prudent thirty miles per hour past the bougainvilleas and poincianas and banyans of Gulfshore Boulevard. He didn't think of the car as stolen, just borrowed, commandeered as a prop in a piece of performance art. He fully intended to give it back before it was missed. He'd be sorry to part with the vehicle, as it felt wonderful sitting behind the oversized burled walnut steering wheel. Still, his plan was to return the car to the lot behind the Third Street shops as soon as it had served its purpose—its purpose being to impress the pants off the young woman he had charmed and bamboozled into driving down from Tallahassee.

Not that the con man even quite knew what he wanted or hoped to get from Renita Daughtry. Sex, sure, if it was offered; but sex was definitely not the final object for Richie Pestucci. In this regard he was quite different from many men, who resorted to elaborate ruses simply to get women into bed; for him, going to bed with a woman was more of a means to an end, the real payoff being in the scam that would eventually follow and that would require a certain level of intimacy and infatuation to succeed.

But what kind of scam? Richie himself never knew at the start. This was part of the fun. A scam was an improvisation that had to be shaped according to the resources of the target. Was she wealthy? Did she have a wonderful car? What was the buying power of her credit cards?

Richie thought Renita probably had a fair amount of dough. In this he was sadly mistaken, though it was an understandable mistake. All he really had to go on was her online profile and the way she'd presented herself in a handful of emails, and the truth is that, while Renita thought of herself as a very honest person, she'd fudged certain details of her resume, sort of tilted things, not so much by what she said but by what she didn't say, a little bit in the direction of grandeur; a little bit toward the life she felt she should have had rather than the life she did. But hey, didn't everybody do that?

So, for instance, she'd alluded to doing a lot of sailing in her childhood, leaving it to the reader to picture gleaming sloops and ketches rather than the leaky, flat-bottomed plywood prams that her father now and then cobbled together and fished from until they sank in the mangroves. She'd casually let slip that she came from an old Florida family that owned a number of properties and was active in politics, but didn't mention that the properties were cramped and weedy lots with cinder-block houses and rusty chain-link fences, or that the politics tended to be those of Mosquito Control or Sewer Maintenance. She didn't lie, she just left a lot of blanks to be filled in, and Richie Pestucci, who as a bullshitter himself should have known better but did not, filled them in with the bullshit of his own desires.

At 8 o'clock sharp, Renita stepped through the front door of the Gulf's Edge Hotel into a balmy and fragrant Naples evening, and two things happened at precisely the same moment: Her phone rang and a gorgeous metallic-blue convertible turned into the driveway.

By reflex, and only for an instant, she looked down at the phone. The call, as she suspected it would be, was from her Uncle Ralph, and she felt a sharp but not entirely unpleasant pang of guilt as she chose to ignore it. Dear Uncle Ralphie. He worried so much about her. Too much, she thought. Phone calls every day, sometimes two or three, monitoring her moods, tickling out her secrets. It was done with love but sometimes it just felt too much like babying. She could take care of herself, thank you very much. Besides, she was entitled to her own adventures, and if she made mistakes now and then and blundered into trouble, what good would worrying do anyway? She turned off the phone and dropped it into her purse and watched the beautiful car pull closer.

It was dusk. There was still just a bit of glare on the windshield, and so there was a delicious moment of suspense before Renita could really make out the features of the man behind the wheel. It turned out he bore a more than passable resemblance to his photo on the dating site. In person, the features were a little more rough-hewn, the black brushy hair a bit more coarse in texture; but hey, didn't everyone touch up their profile picture? Renita decided in a heartbeat that she liked the man's face. Actually, no, she didn't *decide*; what happened was swifter and more visceral than that, a first impression that could never be undone. His face registered as one she would not get tired of looking at. It was sort of diamond-shaped, with very wide-set eyes and a square cleft chin that was undeniably sexy. There was something playful in the very slightly upturning mouth corners, but above all, the man's face struck her as a candid face, an honest face.

The Bentley stopped almost at her feet and the young man sprang out without waiting for the valet to open his door. He moved gracefully around the vehicle to where Renita was standing and reached out a hand to greet her. A handshake. She liked that. It was direct and unassuming. His hand was warm from the steering wheel. He said, "I've been so looking forward to meeting you, Renita. You're even prettier than in your picture."

This may or may not have been true, as her profile shot was also slightly doctored, but in any case Richie Pestucci was not mainly looking at Renita's face or even at her body. He was sizing up her jewelry and her clothes and he was at first glance disappointed, though of course he didn't let it show. Her earrings, while pretty in an artsy-craftsy kind of way, were a little too big and looked like they hadn't cost much. She wore a necklace of some hammered metal that wasn't gold. Her blouse had a little too much flounce and billow to be real silk. Still, he smiled as he said, "Come on, let me show you a little bit of Naples."

That first moment, first smile, first glance had gone on as long as was polite, and he started to look away from her. But Renita, with her disarming habit of holding people's eyes a fraction longer than was usual, didn't quite release his gaze. This intrigued but also slightly flustered Richie. Eye contact was work. It called for the semblance of concentrated honesty, the appearance of unflinching frankness. It was only when he was looking away that he was able to relax, to plan and scheme. This longer locking of eyes was already, by just a tiny increment, throwing off his rhythm.

Still, he gallantly swept her door open and ushered her into the passenger seat. They drove off on whispering tires onto Gulfshore Boulevard. A soft moist breeze tickled Renita's forehead. The leather seat beneath her was like a throne draped over with a cloud. For the moment she was living the life she had imagined and she was very happy. Looking around at the grand houses, the lush landscaping, the arcing parallel palms, she said, "Everything's so perfect here."

Modestly, as though deflecting credit for a personal accomplishment, he said, "It's a nice town."

She said, "More than nice. It's gorgeous. Your family's place is around here?"

He tried to remember exactly what he had told her about the non-existent estate. "Not far," he improvised.

"Can we see it? I'd love to see it."

"I'll take you by sometime," he said. "Unfortunately, we can't go in. Rather a bore, actually. Mother neglected to tell me she was having the termite people come. The house is all closed up for a couple of days."

"Ah, too bad," said Renita. She had no reason to doubt his story. She knew all about subtropical vermin, after all. She said, "So where are you staying?"

"At the yacht club," he said in a rather world-weary tone. In fact he'd been living on a screened porch on the wrong side of town that he'd rented through Airbnb for forty bucks a night. "Pretty basic accommodations. Appalling food. But I have a board meeting later on this evening."

"Tonight?" It struck Renita as a peculiar time to have a meeting, but then she didn't presume to know much about how real yacht clubs worked.

"It's when the Commodore could make it. Flying in from the

Bahamas. I'm sorry, it's just that things get so busy when I'm in town. Besides, I was afraid you might be tired after your drive. I didn't want to press you. We'll have a much fuller day tomorrow. I thought maybe we'd take bicycles up to the Savoy for brunch. Would that be fun?"

The Savoy for brunch! Renita pictured mimosas, flowers on the tables, servers in spotless white tunics, all, of course, against the seamless background of the Gulf. With this considerate and un-pushy man who still had enough of the boy in him that he wanted to ride a bicycle when he could be driving the most beautiful car in the world. She said it sounded lovely, and giggled to herself for using that Victorian word again.

"And maybe for right now a walk on the pier," said her companion. "Quite famous, Naples pier. Quarter-mile long. Dolphins. Pelicans. Feel like a stroll?"

She said a stroll would be just heavenly.

He wondered vaguely if she always talked like that.

10.

In his well-insulated music room in Key West, Pete Amsterdam was trying to listen to Brahms but it just wasn't working for him. He'd focus intently for a while, marveling at the masterful tweaking of the harmonies, the way every nuanced shift within a chord carried with it a different mood, like a sky that alternated between sunshine and a hundred different thicknesses of clouds. He'd track the glorious momentum of a passage climbing and surging toward a climax, tempo quickening, tension building...and then he'd get distracted, and the music, for a few brief but never-to-be-regained seconds, would slip into the background or go unheard altogether.

Very frustrating, those distractions, and exactly the sort of thing that the well-padded and sealed-off music room had been designed to filter out. The ugly whine of scooter engines and the obnoxious honking of their horns; the howls of drunks, the cop car sirens, the accusing rasps of arguing lovers—Key West had a lot of those kinds of noises. Most of them were noises made by other people's problems, and Amsterdam just didn't want to hear them when he was listening to music.

But this was a different kind of distraction, a kind that existed not in the room but inside Pete Amsterdam's head and therefore could not be insulated out. He couldn't quite stop thinking about

Ralphie's niece. No, actually it was Ralphie himself who was the focus and cause of the distraction, because if Ralphie hadn't cared so damn much, then Amsterdam wouldn't either. Such was the power of passionate, unselfish advocacy. Maybe it wasn't surprising that Ralphie cared so much; for him it was family, after all. But the surprising and also, to Amsterdam, the humbling part was how much and how nakedly he let it show, this big, burly, sweaty man who could let himself be brought to the brink of unembarrassed tears with worry for his niece. That kind of caring was contagious, and Amsterdam vaguely knew that he was fighting a losing battle against catching the infection. Well, he told himself, it would probably all turn out just fine; Ralphie's niece would probably be heard from any moment. And he'd be off the hook.

His mind found its way back to the music at last. He caught up with the melody, rewound to the place where his attention had failed him, and tried again to listen.

⚓ ⚓ ⚓

On the pretense of twitching back his sweater cuff, Richie Pestucci stole a quick glance at his wristwatch as he and Renita stepped onto the pier. It was twenty after eight, which meant that everything was right on schedule. Not that the con man had timed the expedition down to the minute. That was not his way. Like most artists, he liked to leave some room to improvise and he also liked to play things near the edge. That's where the adrenaline rush was to be found—in the close calls, the near-disasters, the dicey situations rescued at the buzzer by some cool-headed act of cleverness or chutzpah. If he were playing it safe, he knew he should have the Bentley back by nine-fifteen. Playing it the way he liked to play it, he thought nine-thirty would be fine.

In the meantime they strolled. The wide boards of the pier flexed and squeaked just slightly beneath their feet. It was a starry evening with a bright lopsided moon and the timid little

Gulf waves were flecked and pocked with points of light; water wrapped itself around pilings then pulled away with a wistful whooshing sound. Here and there people were still fishing, arching back to cast, leaning forward intently to retrieve; their catch swam in hopeless circles inside yellow buckets. Old people sat on benches, their hands propped like the paws of sphinxes on their knees.

Richie and Renita walked side by side and only touched when the cadence of their steps made their arms or shoulders briefly brush together or their hips just very lightly graze. Occasionally they walked past pairs of lovers who were pressed against each other's bodies, the pier rail supporting them in their swoon. Some of the lovers were just around Renita's age but they always struck her as younger, and she couldn't say why. Maybe she felt she'd somehow skipped this step of stolen kisses, the tentative parting of unpracticed lips, the clumsy but thrilling embraces; or maybe she hadn't skipped it, just simply missed out on it so far. She wanted to watch the young people hugging but she discreetly looked away. She found herself walking closer to the man at her side, feeling the warmth of his flank against her.

They reached the far end of the pier and turned back to face the distant beach that gleamed an eerie floating silver in the moonlight. Behind it, slowly dancing palms and the spiky triangles of Norfolk pines were silhouetted. Renita said, "Thank you for bringing me here. It's so beautiful."

The con man smiled graciously. "I hoped you'd like it. It's a very special place for me." He looked at his watch again, this time openly, and sighed. "But damn. My meeting. We better be heading back."

Renita didn't want to leave. Not quite so soon. It was a wonderful moment, exactly the kind of moment she'd been starved of, a moment to savor and cling to. Besides, she'd decided there was something that needed to happen and it hadn't happened yet. Stalling for just a little bit more time, angling for her opportunity, she gestured toward the rank of gulf-front mansions that stretched away seemingly without end to the south. "Is one of those your family's house?"

Given such a perfect opening to lie, Richie Pestucci could not, of course, resist. "Yes," he said, and he raised his arm to point vaguely at the imaginary estate. "Can't quite see it from here. It's a ways down…"

He didn't get to finish the lie because just then, while his hand was lifted and his eyes were facing away, Renita leaned in close to him and gave him the softest imaginable kiss on the cheek, a kiss so light it tickled. It was an ambush of a kiss, fleeting, over almost before it could register, a kiss that was at the same time very bold and very bashful, and with an innocent tenderness that excited Richie and also made him feel filthy, low-down, depraved in his duplicity, and absolutely miserable. In his surprise and his sharp but momentary wretchedness, he said, "Why did you do that?"

It might have sounded almost like an accusation but Renita took it as a fair and simple question. "Because you're nice," she said. "Because it's so romantic being here with you. Because you didn't do it first."

The con man couldn't speak just then. He only looked at Renita, looked at her more closely than he had so far, at the translucence of her bright green eyes, the very faint and buried freckles at the sides of her nose, the sensuous grooving of her lips.

Holding his gaze for that disconcerting extra heartbeat, she said, "Do you want to kiss me back? Just once. Just lightly. I'd like it if you did that, Justin."

His stomach soured with a mix of arousal and guilt and he

almost jumped at the sound of his own phony name. He had an impulse to run, to bolt, to barrel down the pier, scattering old ladies if need be, find his way back to the Greyhound station or a freeway on-ramp, and get the hell away from this too-oddly-nice young woman; get the hell away from how he felt. In that sickening moment of utter confusion, an even wilder notion flitted across his mind: maybe he'd drop the pose and tell Renita the truth about himself. That he was a fraud, a fake, that even at that tender moment his main thought was still to find a way to scam her. But the impulse toward confession was banished almost at once. The truth was way too complicated; it would take too long to explain and who could blame Renita if she didn't believe it anyway? So he said nothing and didn't run away. He kissed her on the cheek. The softness of her skin broke his heart a little bit and the pang of his own treachery made him want to bite his face off.

On the stroll back up the pier, she leaned her head against his shoulder. Her hair had a clean smell of mint and papaya. She seemed to be slackening her pace, not walking a straight line, weaving rather dreamily.

Or maybe it just seemed that way to Richie because he was getting seriously worried, secretly panicked almost, about the time. Things were going way too well but taking way too long. This young woman was too trusting, too appealing, too affectionate, and it was lousing everything up. Richie desperately wanted to check his watch again, but the watch was on the arm that Renita was swaying languidly against and he simply couldn't bring himself to break the contact, to push her away. So he meandered at her side, very vaguely understanding that his plans for a scam were being gently but decisively usurped by her imaginings of a romance, and that mooning around at this lover's tempo was probably going to land them both in a hell of a lot of trouble.

11.

It was just after nine pm when Bert the Shirt and Ned Preston rolled out of the Eclipse Saloon. They weren't drunk, but they'd shared a long session of sipping and talking, and the alcohol, in concert with the ripe humidity that had begun to ratchet up as soon as the sun was gone, put a kind of slippery vibrating haze around the streetlamps and a muted Kodachrome sheen on the cars parked underneath them. As soon as they were clear of the tavern's front door, Bert reached down and gently put his chihuahua on the sidewalk. The little dog immediately sauntered over to the curb, went into a hunch, and deposited a pile.

With undisguised pride, Bert said, "Ya see? Ya see? Didn't I tell ya? Every time. No matter what he eats. Attaboy, Nacho. Dog's unbefuckinglievable. Where ya staying? Ya got a hotel?"

The segue from dog poop to lodging was so abrupt that it took Ned a moment to pick up the thread. "No. No hotel. I've been sleeping in the car."

Bert frowned. "Cops hassle ya?"

"Nah, I've been finding some pretty out of the way places. Mangroves, demolition sites."

"Can't be comfortable."

"It's not. Doesn't matter, though. I mean, I've barely slept. Too worried. It's like any minute I'm not out looking for my brother, that's the minute he gets found and whacked. I start to fall asleep, in my mind I see him getting taken out. I wake up wired, have to get up, out of the car, pace around a little."

At that Ned Preston shrugged and yawned. Bert studied him yawning. In recent years he'd noticed a difference between young men and old men in terms of how they got tired. Old men tended to be a little tired to begin with, but increasing fatigue moved in on them only gradually, almost sweetly. They slumped a small notch more, moved even a little slower, became just a tad bit more likely to forget where they were in a story. With young guys, it was different. Young guys could go through a lot—a couple sleepless nights, a beating--without getting tired at all, but when exhaustion finally set in, it set in all at once. Shoulders drooped, eyes went blank, alert and buoyant moods turned punchy or morbid. To Bert it seemed that Ned was on the brink of that right now. He said, "No one sleeps good in a car."

"Doesn't matter. I'll get caught up."

"No you won't. You'll get burned out, you'll feel lousy, you'll make mistakes. Why don't you stay at my place for a night or two?"

"Nah, Bert. Thanks, but with all this going on—"

"I got a couch. Sheets somewhere if I can find 'em. It's no trouble."

"Well, I don't know, that's awfully—"

"On'y thing is, be careful ya don't trip over dog toys. Ya twist an ankle on a rubber hot dog, slip on a chewed-up bone, don't come cryin' to me. Agreed?"

⚓ ⚓ ⚓

Richie Pestucci started up the borrowed Bentley. It took only the slightest nudge of the ignition switch to spark the engine into purring life. The headlights and the dashboard lights came on automatically. The clock read 9:13. There still was time, but not a lot to spare, to bring Renita back to her hotel, say a gracious if hurried goodnight, sealed, perhaps, by a chaste and unaggressive kiss; then to drive like a careening madman back to the Third Street lot, re-park the vehicle, strip off and stash the cotton crew-neck sweater, and be standing calmly at the valet stand in his monogrammed polo by the time the gorgeous convertible was reclaimed. It would be close but he liked to play things close. He put the car in gear.

Renita was still settling slowly, languorously, into the all-over embrace of the passenger seat. A seat as splendidly comfortable as that, you didn't just plop down on; you eased in, feeling the supple leather yield and shape itself against your butt and legs and shoulder blades. Nor was there any big hurry to yank the seat belt into place. She took a moment to settle the strap just so between her breasts, and as she was snapping the buckle she said, "Do you think we could take a quick look at your family's house? Just from the outside, I mean?"

Richie bit his lip and said, "Um, why not tomorrow? In daylight. When we're on our bicycles."

Renita didn't pout but she didn't try too hard to hide her disappointment either. She said, "Oh, I just thought it would be so nice to see it in moonlight. When you were pointing toward it from the pier, there was such, oh, I don't know, such affection in your eyes. I tried to imagine how many wonderful memories the place must hold for you."

Richie tried to smile but his lips caught on his teeth. They were just approaching the stop sign at the intersection of 12th Avenue South and Gulfshore Boulevard. A right turn would take them northward, directly toward Renita's hotel. A left would take them south toward Port Royal and the non-existent family estate. It was 9:17.

Renita went on. "And I was thinking about how the places we're from, they shape us, kind of steer us toward being the people we are. The person *you* are. Charming. Gentle. Earnest."

Richie turned left.

He felt he had to, though he didn't quite know why. He had no intention of falling in love with this relentlessly romantic and strangely off-the-beat young woman. He doubted by now that she was rich or that winning her trust and stealing her checkbook would amount to much of a score. Yet he found himself playing along with her gauzy version of what a great first date should be, indulging her every whim. Why? Maybe he was simply courting doom, as he habitually seemed to do. Or maybe her starry-eyed musings were turning out to be the perfect answer, the antidote, to his bullshit. Or maybe he just liked her more than he knew how to handle.

In any case, he drove and the seconds ticked away. Gulfshore Boulevard folded into Gordon Drive and the houses grew even grander, sprouted turrets and towers; the gates and hedges grew ever taller, more imposing, more enveloping. Not knowing this privileged precinct very well, Richie scanned the road ahead, past gnarled enormous banyans and overarching oaks, trying to decide which grandiose residence he could get away with claiming as his own. Finally he chose one more or less at random as the clock notched forward to 9:24.

The property was sealed off by a vast and flawless bank of

purple bougainvillea and not much of the house itself could be seen until the Bentley pulled even with the driveway, which was flanked by a pair of huge stone lions and blocked off by a tall wrought iron railing. From that vantage, Renita saw a palatial villa that didn't exactly look like Tuscany but rather like a very high-budget movie pretending to be set in Tuscany. "My God," she said, "it's beautiful. Magnificent."

Richie only smiled modestly. He hadn't even put the car in Park, let alone switched off the ignition. His plan had been to give Renita one quick look at the dark and empty mansion then turn around and get the hell out of there.

To his chagrin, though, she'd already unbuckled her seat belt and was opening the passenger door. She fairly floated out of the car. There was something disembodied, boneless, in her movements, as if she wasn't willing herself to move but rather had been swept up in some soft-focus dream scenario that could not be resisted. She wafted to the iron railing and struck a classically wistful pose—her pale hands wrapped around the black metal spikes of the gate, her face squeezed between the bars as she gazed at the unattainable house.

Richie called out from the car. "Renita, we really need to go."

He tried to keep the edge out of his voice, to sound as gracious and easy as he'd sounded all evening, to squelch any note of frustration or tension, but apparently he failed at that, because when Renita turned back toward him there was just a slight hint of hurt or letdown in her face, a faint suggestion that this too perfect evening had now received its first small scuff. "What?" she said. "Is something wrong?"

12.

"**M**an, this stuff is cool," said Ned Preston, as he looked around Bert's compact and rather cluttered condo at such curiosities as a wired phone with a curvaceous handset and molded plastic base; a hi-fi whose radio dial was connected to a pointer that moved in a track all the way from 88 to 107; a formica dinette table edged in red and stamped with a design of flying boomerangs. "It's like an antique shop in here."

Bert said nothing to that, just put Nacho on the floor. The dog immediately attacked a squeak toy made to look like a miniature pepperoni pizza.

"In a good way, I mean," Ned went on. "Hope it didn't come out wrong."

His host didn't seem to be offended. He said mildly, "Lived here forty years. Fifteen with my late wife. Twenty-five on my own. Never felt the need to change much. Stuff still works."

Ned just nodded while admiring a light fixture modeled after Sputnik.

"Been a long time since I had a houseguest, though," the old man mused. "Interesting, tryin' to see the place through someone else's eyes. Must look like a tomb to you."

"No, I wouldn't say—"

"It's okay, I get it. Young people, they see all this dusty out-of-date stuff, it's kind of hard for them to imagine that the people whose stuff it is used to be young too. Hard to imagine there were great times here. But there were."

As he said this, he was staring through the passageway between the living room and kitchen and picturing his wife in there, wearing an apron with a pattern of tumbling pots and pans in blue and green. She was humming while she made a *pannetone*, the real Sicilian kind, eggy, not too sweet, studded with dried fruit. The oven was heating, the kitchen smelled of cinnamon and browning butter. Opera was on the radio.

"We always had music on," Bert remembered. "Very musical, my wife. Loved to sing."

At that, the dog dropped the plastic pizza and launched into its three-note howl. *Ow-ow-OWWW. Ow-ow-OWWW.* The baying brought Bert out of his reverie. "Christ, Nacho. Not now."

To Ned, he said, "What would you say to a nightcap? A little anisette?"

🏝 🏝 🏝

It was 9:28 when Renita got back in the car. This time she didn't make a ceremony of settling into the luxurious seat, just slid in and pulled the door shut behind her. As she was fastening her seat belt, her companion said, "I hope I didn't sound abrupt."

"No, no," said Renita. "My fault. Your meeting. I know you have a meeting."

They both tried to smile, to put this first tiny tiff behind them. Richie worked hard at seeming calm and gracious. He made a sweeping but not hurried U-turn and headed back north in the direction of Renita's hotel.

Feeling that everything was okay again between them, she reached out softly and touched his hand as it rested on the steering wheel. "I'm so looking forward to tomorrow," she said. "Biking up the beach. What a perfect idea."

He half-turned toward her as he drove and attempted another generous smile. When he tried to pull his eyes back toward the road, Renita held them for that extra fraction. The clock read 9:33. Richie heard a faraway siren.

Renita heard it also, but, clear of conscience, made nothing of it whatsoever. To her it was just a random night-sound, background noise, filler on the soundtrack.

Richie, though, was secretly transfixed. He cocked an ear and tried to gauge the distance of the sound, the direction it was coming from. He tried to imagine that the sound was growing fainter but he knew deep down it wasn't. He could feel the adrenaline starting to spread its frozen heat through his arms and legs, though he was still a notch or two away from panic.

Renita, thinking joyfully ahead to the next day's planned adventure, said, "What's your favorite thing for brunch? I think mine's probably French toast. With Canadian bacon."

Richie pretended to be thinking it over. He wasn't. He was listening to the siren. A second one had just joined in chorus with the first, and their wavering, intertwining music, though still a long way off, began inexorably to rise in volume. In the con man's mind, over the course of an anguished fifteen or twenty seconds, denial was steadily giving way to a resignation heavily tinged with self-mockery. The Bentley had probably by now been missed and traced, and he was screwed. The part that gnawed at him was that he'd screwed himself. He'd screwed himself by deviating from his plan, losing control of the agenda and the timing. He'd spent too many moments looking back at Renita's green eyes. He'd dawdled and returned her silly little kiss. Stupidly, he'd let himself be charmed by her romantic gushing, let himself become a mere chauffeur and prop in her glamorous night out, and now the cops were after him.

"Shit," he muttered.

The mild expletive was neither loud nor threatening but it was so at odds with his previously courtly language that Renita, without taking time to really think about it, instantly began to be a little bit afraid. "What, Justin?" she said. "What is it?"

He didn't answer. He just drove and listened to the sirens. Their wails were dopplering higher and there was no longer any doubt that they were moving toward him. Suddenly seized by a blind and guilty imperative to flee, he swerved and hung another U-turn, this time a ferocious one that spit gravel from the road shoulder and bit deeply into the sod of someone's lawn. Tires screeched, the big car leaned and lurched then finally found its equilibrium as it barreled beneath the tunneling trees and past the gloomy statuary of Port Royal. Mansions zipped past in a blur. Foliage that had been still as a painting was whipped into sudden frenzy by the fierce draft of the speeding vehicle.

Renita clutched her armrest, pressed herself back against her seat, and tried without any chance of success to understand what had so abruptly changed, to isolate the moment when the evening's fairy tale had seamlessly crossed over into nightmare and her suave companion had started acting like a madman. "Justin," she said. "Talk to me, please. Why are you doing this?"

Richie just pressed down on the accelerator.

13.

Sipping anisette at the table with the boomerang motif, Bert said to his guest, "Mind if I ask you something? This job you said you have, this pumping cappuccino, zat really what you wanna do?"

"It's not bad," said Ned.

"Didn't say it was. But a young guy like you, you seem pretty presentable and all, I thought maybe you'd be aiming at something...something...ya know..."

"Better?" Ned rescued him. "It's all right. You can say it. Sure I'd like a better job. Not easy finding one these days. Especially since I never finished college."

"Ah. Ya didn't like it?"

"Actually, I loved it. Ran out of money junior year."

"Parents couldn't help?"

"My father died young. Left nothing."

"School loans? Anything like that?"

Ned looked down at the table, picked up one of the *biscotti* that Bert had put there on a flower-pattern plate, and said, "Yeah, I had loans. And a little savings. Pretty much just enough. Used it to post bail for my brother first time he got arrested. He skipped."

Bert broke off a corner of a *biscotto* and fed it to the dog. "That kinda sucks."

Ned said nothing to that, just sipped some anisette and felt its licorice sweetness drawing at his gums.

"He ever pay ya back, at least?"

"Seems to have slipped his mind these last half dozen years or so."

Not quite realizing he was speaking aloud, Bert said, "Bad news, this guy."

"Look, you don't get to pick who you share a uterus with. I'm awfully tired, Bert. Mind if we turn in?"

The old man was grateful for the suggestion. He rose slowly from the table and led the way down a narrow corridor to look for bedclothes. The linen closet door had swollen with humidity and it stuck. With difficulty he pulled it open to reveal neat shelves of towels rubbed largely bare of their terry loops and pastel sheets that had not been used in many years. They gave off a stale yet somehow welcoming smell of mildew and detergent and a not quite floral, not quite spicy tang from the kind of sachet that old ladies always put in linen closets. Gesturing toward a high shelf, Bert said, "Those should work for the sofa. Help yourself."

Ned reached up toward the stack of sheets and pillowcases. They seemed heavier than they should have been. As he lifted them, something dark and hard slipped out from the middle of the pile and landed with a thud in the thick shag of the carpet. It was a snub-nosed .38 in serious need of a buffing and with a few deep scratches on its stubby barrel.

Bert looked down at it and said very casually, "Shit, so *that's* where I put it. Couldn't remember for the life a me."

Without trying to conceal the effort it cost him, the old man bent low to retrieve the gun, then straightened up slowly and tucked it into the gapping waistband of his pants. "Never know when it might come in handy. Well, nighty-night. Bathroom's over there. Sweet dreams."

🌴 🌴 🌴

Speeding along in the overdue Bentley, thinking now of nothing but escape, Richie Pestucci, new to town, failed to understand that Naples was in fact an island and that he was very quickly coming to the end of it.

Second by second the land was narrowing, pinching in. Trees were growing sparser, lonelier. Shrubbery was dwarfed in the thin and sandy soil. Deep-dug canals branched off from the edge of the road; tidy wooden bulkheads framed alleyways of sea. Pleasure boats were asleep on davits or nestled against the pilings of private docks.

A couple of hundred yards ahead, Gordon Drive just stopped. There was no fanfare, no barrier, just a modest and dusty cul de sac with a cramped turnaround marked by a faded arrow.

Richie slammed on the brakes. There was a screech, then the grinding hiss of a skid, then the car was still and everything was marvelously quiet except for the whine of the sirens perhaps a mile up the road. Renita wasn't crying, not exactly, but the outside edges of her eyes were moist and stinging from the salt wind that had been slapping at her in the open car. She said, "Justin, what the hell is going on?"

By reflex he stalled for time while awaiting inspiration for a credible lie. All he said was, "Well, we've run into a little problem."

Renita had been shaken out of her romantic trance by then, and her elevated diction came back down to earth. "Yeah, I picked up on that. What kind of problem?"

The sirens were getting louder. There were beginning to be crazy flashes in the canopies of distant trees from the patrol cars' veering high-beams.

He said, "There isn't time to explain right now." He swiveled quickly toward her, a look of utter candor in his wide-set eyes. "Renita, listen, do you trust me?"

"Like, right now? At this moment? Not really. Why should I?"

"Because I'm asking you to."

"I don't think that's enough of a reason."

"Because I need you to. Because there are things I haven't told you. I will, I promise. But for right now you need to make a choice, and you need to make it fast. Leave or stay."

"Leave?" she said, gesturing vaguely at the empty night around her. "Get out here in the middle of nowhere?"

"Or stay with me and take your chances."

"My chances with what? What's going to happen?"

"Beyond the next couple of minutes? I really couldn't tell you."

The police cars were now close enough that their spinning

roof-lights sent fleeting smears of ugly red through gaps in the nighttime foliage.

She said, "This is getting to be one strange date."

"Look at me, Renita. Look at me and make up your mind."

She stared at him hard, at the face she'd decided, probably too quickly, that she liked and wouldn't tire of looking at. There was torment in that face now; at least that's how she read it. There was need. He wasn't forcing her to do one thing or another. He was asking her to choose. He was inviting her to an adventure, a different set of possibilities. It was up to her to go along or not. She heard a voice say, "Okay, I'm in." She realized it had been her voice.

He said, "You should probably undo your seat belt."

"Seat belt?"

That was all she had time to say. Richie Pestucci wheeled around the cul de sac, floored the Bentley for maximum momentum, and wrenched the steering wheel toward the nearest canal. The car roared, bucked, and sprang up the small embankment. The big tires compressed and rebounded against the hard edge of the bulkhead, and the convertible took flight, seeming to arch in mid-air like a steeplechase horse, rising, leveling, then tipping down toward impact. The front fender hit first, the broad chassis following in an epic belly-flop. Wide and tortured ripples surged outward from the impact and in less than three seconds the water was above the top edge of the windshield and the borrowed Bentley had simply disappeared.

PART TWO

14.

The water was slippery and almost warm. It came cascading over the doors of the sinking car like an intimate Niagara, and even before Renita had begun to thrash and struggle it was already pooling underneath her and lifting her out of her seat. Almost peacefully, she bobbed upward toward air and moonlight, and when she reached the surface and gulped in a hungry breath, Richie Pestucci's streaming face was very close to hers. He asked if she could swim.

The question for some reason struck her funny. No doubt she was in shock, hyper-alert yet also strangely, blessedly numb. "You might have asked me that before."

"You're right. I should have. Sorry."

They treaded water above the sunken convertible. The ripples from its sinking were pretty much already gone. So much for a drowned Bentley, just one more wreck for fish to play around in. The sirens were punishingly loud by now, their accusing sound seeming to skid and scratch across the water.

Renita said, a little petulantly, "Of course I can swim. I'm from Key West, remember?"

He nodded, then took her by the wrist, not gently, not roughly, somewhere in the enormous middle ground between ordering and pleading. She said, "Justin, why'd you sink the car?"

"I'll explain that soon. I promise."

It was hard to tread water with just one hand so she pulled her arm away. "It was stolen, wasn't it?"

Richie needed zero time to think about his answer. He spat out a lie by reflex, the way a frog flicks out its tongue to catch a fly. "Stolen? Of course it wasn't stolen. It's my car, Renita. You think I'm happy about losing it? I had to. There wasn't any choice. They're after me."

"Who? Who's after you?"

The sirens abruptly stopped then. Two police cars, having finally reached the cul de sac, braked hard and rocked to a halt. Richie shook some water from his thick black hair and spoke in a hoarse whisper. "Renita, *please*."

He said nothing else, just stared at her for one more instant then swam away. Kicking silently, most of him below the surface, he slid toward an edge of the canal where he'd be hidden by the wavy shadows of pilings and yachts.

For a moment Renita watched his slow but steady progress outward toward the broad estuary that led on to the Gulf. Vaguely, her thoughts in a messy and unsorted heap, not really thoughts at all, just a jumble of hopes and fears, she considered her options. She could swim after him. Or she could tread water where she was, confront the cops, trust that they wouldn't shoot her, and try to explain the business of the sunken car, not to mention the absence of anyone but her who might have sunk it. That would be awkward. Also, she was dimly wondering about all the questions that would go unanswered if she never again saw the appealing and completely puzzling man with whom she'd spent the evening. How big a loss would that be? Would it be a loss at all? She thought about her dull life in Tallahassee, her boring classes, studying psychology from books but not from life. She thought about her unlived adventures that she knew deep down were only daydreams and that before tonight had never put on flesh and gone capering through moonlight. She hoped that what she felt herself deciding was a real decision and not a giving in to some kind of exciting but slightly crazy thrall.

She started swimming after him.

It was a short swim to the junction of the canal with the estuary known as the Gordon River, then an easy float of a couple hundred yards on a falling tide to where the river shoaled up at its mouth and a breakwater of enormous, jagged boulders protected the extremely high-priced beach. Getting over the sharp and looming rocks was the hard part; like scaling a miniature mountain range in darkness.

Renita's backless shoes had slipped off long before and narrow crevices between the boulders grabbed and bit at her feet. Richie's sodden cotton sweater had grown so heavy that he could barely lift his arms to clamber; he peeled it off and left it on a rock. Sometimes the two of them jumped from crag to crag; sometimes they crawled. By the time they'd topped the breakwater and threaded their way down along the inshore side, their limbs were trembling with fatigue and as soon as their feet found the salvation of soft sand they let themselves collapse down onto it in the time-honored manner of castaways.

Renita lay there and took a moment to catch her breath and take stock of her peculiar situation. Only then, back on land, did she seem to notice that she didn't have her purse, that it had been left behind in the sunken Bentley. The purse held her wallet, driver's license, credit cards, a student-sized amount of cash. These were piddling losses but the purse had also held her phone, which had no doubt been pickled and shorted out by salt water. The loss of the phone, for a person who never since girlhood had been without one, was not so much devastating as simply inconceivable, dizzying. She was suddenly cut off from the world. She couldn't reach anyone; nobody could reach her. She was as untethered and alone as if she'd flown up to the moon.

The thought was terrifying and also very bracing.

It was also somehow chilling; it made her notice that the evening had grown quite cool and that her dripping, clammy clothes made it even cooler. The fringes and flounces of her blouse held a burdensome amount of water. Her skirt was beribboned with seaweed and caked with sand and lay rumpled around her like the flag of a defeated country. She realized she'd be much more comfortable in bare skin that would have a chance to dry. Without ceremony, completely matter-of-factly, she stood up and starting stripping down to her underwear.

Richie Pestucci watched her while pretending not to. Her underwear was very chaste and simple, less revealing than many bathing suits; still, it was underwear, and the mere idea of it held titillation.

Renita, damp, pearly, tall and gorgeous in the moonlight, and not just then feeling the slightest bit romantic, made it clear that her scanty attire was neither tease nor come-on. "Purely a practical matter," she said. "And I'm still waiting for some explanations."

"Fine, sure," he said, "but we better start walking. I'm guessing it's about three miles up to your hotel."

"Who are we running away from, Justin?"

Of course he dodged the question. "Look, it won't take them long to find the car. They'll drag the canal, they'll send a diver down. And then they'll be after us."

"Us? I haven't done anything."

"Look, they'll be after anyone who was in the car. Think about it, Renita. What'll they do? They'll look for stuff. Anything that might have ID on it. Anything of yours still in the car?"

For a moment she just stood there in her bra and panties, goose bumps on her neck and shoulders, toes curled with perturbation in the cool sand, ruined skirt and blouse dangling heavily from one hand. She didn't answer the question. She didn't have to.

In one smooth movement the con man got to his feet and started moving. "Come on," he said, "we'll stay ahead of them."

15.

"Special Ops," he was saying.

They'd been walking up the moonlit, estate-lined beach for maybe half an hour and he'd had time to concoct at least the bare bones of a story.

"Afghanistan," he said. "Remember the team of Navy Seals that finally nailed Bin Laden? Big heroes, right? Well, you think those were the only guys out looking? They weren't. No way. There were multiple teams. I couldn't tell you exactly how many because it was very hush-hush. Top secret. We weren't even supposed to know about each other."

"Ah. So you were on one of the other teams?" Renita asked.

Richie smiled to himself. He loved it that she had jumped in with a question. People tended to put more credence in a story that they themselves had helped to tell. Caught up in his yarn, though, he didn't quite catch the hint of skepticism in her voice.

"Yes," he answered. "Exactly. I was on a different team. In the mountains. We didn't catch Bin Laden but we caught somebody else. Somebody, unfortunately, we were not supposed to catch."

They walked. The tide was out and thin brittle shells crunched under their feet at the water's edge. Richie had rolled his pants legs up; his polo shirt had almost dried. At un-self-conscious moments Renita nearly forgot that she was strolling in her undies. At other moments she saw herself as though from the perspective of a stranger watching and was visited by fleeting and not entirely unpleasant little spasms of shock and shame. "So who did you catch?" she asked.

Rather absurdly, Richie peered around the empty nighttime beach and the vacant Gulf of Mexico before he answered almost in a whisper. "A member of the Saudi royal family. Working with ISIS. A renegade, but apparently a beloved renegade. Young. Handsome. Misguided, I guess the family thought. We captured him, held him a week, then mysteriously were ordered to release him and delete all reference to the capture from the logs. Three choppers showed up in the middle of nowhere and carried him away. Very respectful. VIP treatment start to finish."

"And that was the end of it?" Renita asked.

"More like the beginning," he replied. "There were six guys on our team. Within the next month, five of them were killed. Skirmishes, they said. Too much coincidence for me. I had the feeling it was friendly fire. As in assassination. I sneaked into a Red Cross convoy about a hundred miles outside Kabul. Eventually made my way back to the States by way of Switzerland."

"So you deserted?"

"I was never *in*. That's the point, Renita. All of this was unofficial, technically illegal. I had no protection. But I figured I was safe here in the U.S. No one would want to risk a scandal, a political blow-up. But if those people catch me—"

"*What* people, Justin?"

"The Saudis," he said, as though it should be obvious. "Their agents. Those people chasing us—you think they were regular cops?"

"Well...uh...yeah. Sirens and all. Spinning lights on top."

"No way they were regular cops. Saudi agents. They catch me, I'll be bundled into a plane, taken to the Middle East, and never be heard from again. That's why I can't let myself be cornered. That's why I had to ditch the car. Do you understand now?"

What she understood—what she *thought* she understood by now—was that she was dealing with a very resourceful, flaming, and inveterate liar. A textbook liar, even. Seeing him in action was, perversely, a kind of privilege, but that still left the question of how she should respond. Considering, she looked off at the fuzzy seam of the horizon and at the gauzy globes of orange mist that throbbed around the dim lights of the Naples pier. They were quite close to the pier by now, to the place where this bewildering adventure had begun—amazingly—barely over two hours before. At the time it had seemed like an idyll that should be painted in pastels and backed by violins. Somehow it had turned into...what? As much as anything, the evening had become a tug-of-war between belief and disbelief.

Renita had never before had cause to notice how many fine and edgeless gradations there were between the two; belief was as fuzzy as the lights out on the pier. Until tonight, she'd thought you believed something or you didn't. Now she was realizing that you could choose to believe. You could prefer to believe. You could play at believing when really you didn't. You could pretend to believe, and dare another person to believe you really did. That was the surprise: that belief didn't happen all inside your head but was a dynamic, a game between two people. Believing was a pact, and not always a holy or a healthy one; believing was a kind of conspiracy.

After a long pause, Renita said, "So let me make sure I have this right. Your name is Justin. You have family here in Naples. That beautiful car was really yours. And you drove it into the canal because Saudi spies are after you. Do I have it straight?"

"Yes, you do. I know it's all very strange, Renita, but life is like that sometimes, much stranger than a person could make up."

"I understand," she said. "I really do." She stood there for a moment in her undies in the moonlight, her feet being tickled by the last foamy tendrils of tiny waves, and then she added, "But Justin, can I ask you one more thing? Why does it say Gregory on your shirt?"

16.

In Key West, Pete Amsterdam had gone to bed early because of a slightly neurotic suspicion that he wasn't going to sleep well anyway, so he ought at least to get a head start on the night. That's how things tended to go for him when he had other people's problems on his mind. The strange part was that his own problems seldom rendered him sleepless. Those, he knew how to deal with; he could save their solutions for another day. But other people's problems seemed to come at him with greater urgency and in unfamiliar, haunting, goblin-like forms; other people's problems pulled sheets over their heads and wandered through his nighttime mind like cartoon ghosts.

So he tossed and turned and wondered if Ralphie's niece was really in danger or if she was just a little nutty. If she'd put herself in the clutches of a true predator, or if she was just tired of feeling like she was missing out on life, just treating herself to a bit of risky fun. What was that old Beatles lyric? *When you find yourself in the thick of it, help yourself to a bit of what is all around you.* Problem was, the thick of it was where bad things tended to happen.

So the thoughts chased each other round and round, and Amsterdam didn't sleep much.

It was not yet full daylight when he was yanked out of a doze by the repeated ringing of his doorbell and a determined pounding on his front door that sent faint tremors all through the old frame house. Almost grateful to have the bad night ended, he rolled out of bed and pulled on a bathrobe, then, eyes itching and mouth dry, he trundled down the stairs and opened the front door.

Ralphie was standing on the far side of the threshold, backed by the pallid yellow light of dawn, enveloped in the sweetish funk of the day's first flowers struggling to open. He looked like hell. His eyes were bloodshot, his hair was matted, his jowls sagged in purple folds. He seemed to have slept in his clothes, or more likely not. He said, "Can I come in?"

Without waiting for an answer he leaned past Amsterdam and lurched into the house. When he'd made it to the same living room chair he'd sat in the evening before, he blurted out, "They found her."

"Found her?" Amsterdam echoed numbly.

"Up in Naples. Found her stuff, at least. Purse. IDs. Cops contacted her parents around three o'clock this morning."

Amsterdam said, "Lemme make some coffee."

He went off to the kitchen. In his heart he knew he was hiding in there, fending off news of a tragedy, wondering what lame words of comfort he would offer if something truly terrible had happened. He took his time pouring in milk.

When he finally handed a steaming mug to Renita's uncle, the big man said, "Her purse was in a fancy car. Sunk in a canal."

"Sunk?"

"Sunk. Apparently on purpose. After a chase. Stolen."

"Stolen by?"

The big man shrugged. "I guess by the asshole she was going there to meet. Prince Charming. Mr. Wrong. But they didn't find anything of his. Only hers. Typical, right?"

Amsterdam took a sip of coffee and braced himself. "Have they...?" he began, but then he couldn't quite get himself to ask the brutal question.

Ralphie had more courage. "Dredged? Yeah, supposedly they've dredged. No bodies. My niece wouldn't drown. She was always a real water baby. She wouldn't drown."

Amsterdam knocked wood in a way he hoped the other man wouldn't notice. Then he said, "Cops know anything more? They say anything else to the parents?"

"They asked if their daughter knew a man named Gregory Sanderson-Simes."

"Who the hell is that?"

"That's what they asked too. Apparently he's a valet parker in Naples," Ralphie said. "At least that's the name he put down on his job application. Probably phony. Social security number didn't check out. He's the guy that parked the car. Almost definitely the guy that stole it, the guy Renita was with."

Amsterdam sipped some coffee and begged his mind to clear. "Wait a sec," he said. "The guy she was going to meet. Didn't you tell me his name was Justin?"

"Justin, right. That's what she told me. Except now it's Gregory. Same guy, apparently. Different names. Probably both fake."

The groggy detective looked out the window. It framed a rectangle of light that was changing quickly now from a hazy ecru to a searing white. "Bear with me," he said. "So it turns out Renita got her hopes way up and drove all the way from Tallahassee to Naples to have a first date with a valet parker?"

"What can I say?" her uncle replied. "She thought he was rich and artsy and well-traveled and a gentleman. She thought it would be wonderful. She was trusting her instincts, remember?"

17.

Bert the Shirt, as he did nearly every morning, had gone out very early to get a paper from the pay-box just across A1A. He timed it so he could see the sun come up from out beyond Stock Island; seeing sunrise through the sailboat masts and behind the coursing pelicans was at least a partial compensation for being a lousy sleeper anyway. He also liked it that, at that hour in Key West, he felt no compunction about going out in his pajamas and monogrammed bathrobe of royal blue satin, its fraying tasseled belt knotted loosely where his appendix used to be. He'd gathered up his excited little dog, which promptly dropped a load at curbside, then wandered over to the pay-box that was almost completely plastered over with handbills, graffiti, and wishful-thinking drawings of jumbo male and female genitalia. Luckily for Bert, he got there just as the driver was putting in the papers and was able to glom one for free.

He brought it upstairs to the condo and found Ned Preston still sleeping soundly on the living room sofa. He padded softly to the kitchen in his scuffed-up slippers and made himself an espresso. By the time he heard his houseguest stirring he'd had a second cup and read the paper front to back. He put the pot back on the stove and made some coffee for Ned.

When he delivered it, the young man was wrestling rather ineffectually with the twisted bedclothes on the cramped and unfamiliar couch. There was something touching in the spectacle of his sleepy helplessness, something somehow overgrown or past its expiration date, as if he were a college grad who'd been forced to move back home to a bed no longer big enough. Bert handed him a demi-tasse and asked him how he'd slept.

"Really well. Terrific. Thanks." He sipped some coffee and continued squirming under the tangled sheet.

Bert then slapped the newspaper, which was opened to page three. "If you're awake enough to think straight, there's a little item here I thought might be of more than passing interest or let's say *a propos*. Gregory Sanderson-Simes. That name ring a bell?"

Ned said it didn't.

"One of your brother's aka's by any chance?" the old man pressed.

Ned ran a hand through his mat of thick black hair. "Not one I've heard before. Then again, sort of sounds like one of his. He has a thing for hyphens. Guess they make him sound aristocratic. Why?"

Bert said, "Well, this particular purported or let's say would-be aristocrat is alleged to have stolen a Bentley up in Naples and eluded capture by driving into the drink."

"Naples?" said Ned, still wrestling with the bedclothes. "But my brother isn't in Naples."

"Says you," countered Bert, pulling on his long lower lip. "But I got a theory or maybe better to call it a whaddyacallit, inference, based on several points. Point A: Everybody's gotta be somewhere. Point B: You and a bunch of killers haven't been able to find him in Key West, which, let's face it, is a pretty dinky place, which suggests he ain't here. Point C: This fake name and stolen car bit is starting to sound pretty familiar as your brother's M.O."

Ned wavered on the brink of buying it but still resisted. "It's not like he has a monopoly on stealing cars."

"True," Bert conceded. Then he held the newspaper at arm's length and squinted to read some lines. "And he doesn't have a monopoly on being Caucasian, around twenty-eight years old, with short black hair, prominent cheekbones, around five-eleven with an athletic build."

"Shit," said Ned. He sipped his coffee and stared down at the tormented sheets before adding resignedly, "They catch him?"

"Not according to this. Cops are seeking information. They think maybe there's an accomplice."

Ned shook his head at that. "Very doubtful. That isn't how he operates. There's never an accomplice. Doesn't trust anyone enough to take on an accomplice."

"Be that as it may," said Bert, "says here they found some IDs in the car. Belonging to a person of the feminine persuasion named Renita Daughtry. Ring a bell?"

"Not at all."

"Twenty-two. Student at Florida State. But here's the part I thought was kind of interesting. Permanent address is in Key West."

The caffeine hadn't quite made it into Ned's bloodstream yet and all he said was, "Kind of a funny coincidence."

"Coincidence, yeah," said Bert. "Funny, we shall see."

"Where you going with this?" Ned asked.

"Going? Who knows? Maybe nowhere. But I been thinking or let's say mulling this over while you were still off in dreamland. What do we know about this young female individual named Renita Daughtry? Who is she? Accomplice? Squeeze? Scam target? Good person? Bad person? We don't know squat."

"So far we agree," Ned put in dryly.

"But here's the thing," Bert said, "that I believe might possibly matter or be of consequence even in spite of your dubious tone and hint of sarcasm which by the way I did detect and not especially appreciate. Okay, we don't know who she is. But put yourself in her shoes. You're twenty-two years old. You've had a scare. You've lost your stuff and probably your money. You're in trouble. You're four hundred miles away from where you go to school but only two hundred from the bosom of your family. Where you gonna go?"

Ned had finally thrashed his way out of the cocoon of sheets and, more alert now, was sitting on the sofa in his jockey shorts. "So you think she's coming here?"

"All I'm saying is that I think it's a reasonable surmise and possibly even how a person might actually act to think that maybe she'd look to Mom and Dad for a hug and some cash, and to do that she might put in an appearance at...Where the hell did that address go?" He squinted again at the paper until the print came into focus. "At 1819 Jamaica Drive. I'm gonna guess that's where her parents live."

The con man's brother was pressing his lips together and looking down at the hair on his legs. Sounding pessimistic now to pre-empt a disappointment later, he said, "I don't know. Seems logical. But even if she came down here I don't think my brother'd be with her. That's not his way. Things go wrong, he bolts. Alone."

"Bolts in what?" asked Bert the Shirt.

"Excuse me?"

"I mean, based on what we know so far and the various mishaps and piss-poor decisions that have brought us to this junction or maybe juncture the word is, I think it's fair to say that your brother right now, and I'm trying to put this tactfully, is between vehicles."

"And this Renita person has a car?"

"Says right here," said Bert. "Police are looking for a car registered to her, a green 2004 Nissan sedan."

At that Ned Preston couldn't resist a mirthless laugh that rattled his coffee cup. "An '04 Nissan sedan? My brother wouldn't be caught dead in an '04 Nissan sedan."

Bert said, "Well, let's hope it doesn't come to that."

Ned stopped laughing quickly.

"You and me," the old man went on, "you think we're the only people who look at the police blotter? Come on, it's the best part of the paper. Marco and his guys, I mean, I doubt they're big readers, but it's only natural to be curious about your friends and colleagues. You think they don't check out the crime stuff?"

18.

Bert's guesswork was pretty close to right. In fact, if things had gone as planned, he would have had them nailed. But things didn't go as planned. Things hardly ever did.

Back in Naples, it had been close to midnight when Richie and Renita finished their long moonlit slog back to her hotel. She'd slithered once again into her dank and clammy clothing, gone into the lobby by way of the poolside entrance, and endured the disapproving stare of the desk clerk as he handed her a duplicate key to her room. Upstairs, she took a hurried shower—but not so hurried that she didn't take a moment to consider whether or not she would fulfill her promise to pick up her companion a block away, where he'd decided it would be more prudent to hide out in the shadow of a towering rank of oleanders.

But why should she pick him up? Why not take this opportunity to get clear of him and flee?

She had a car. He didn't. Why shouldn't she just drive away and leave him standing there? Or maybe even go to the police, since she herself had done nothing wrong so far, whereas he'd stolen a pricey convertible, destroyed it, risked drowning both of them, and fled the scene. He'd been nothing but trouble. Then again, that wasn't exactly true. He'd been trouble but not *only* trouble. He'd also been at moments gentle and considerate, and always fascinating.

Honest? Not so much. Special ops? Saudi agents? Please. The wrong name on the polo shirt was the final straw. A mix-up at the dry cleaners? That was pretty lame. Who had polo shirts dry-cleaned anyway?

But if Renita no longer bought the spiel, why was she still playing at believing him? Why was she choosing to remain a voluntary captive in the ever more entangling web that he was spinning? Was it just physical attraction, simply that she liked his face? Or was it getting to be as much about research as romance? Psych major meets sociopath--a senior thesis waiting to happen. Questions to be addressed: How much did the subject really expect to be believed? How much did he even *want* to be believed? What would it take to get him to drop the mask, and what would one see if he did?

Mulling, wavering, but probably not wavering as much as she should have, she pulled on dry clothes, gathered together her few remaining things, called the valet for her car, and went to pick him up.

She had no way of knowing that, for him too, it had come pretty close to a coin toss as to whether he'd be there waiting for her or if he would have lit out on his own.

His feelings were no less complex than hers. A few hours ago, Renita had been a mark and nothing more. He'd meant to steal her credit cards, hopefully some passwords, possibly her whole identity. If he got laid in the process, so much the better.

But then there'd been that weird and wholly unexpected kiss out on the pier; and her over-the-top romantic musings that made him feel like the dirtiest dog in the world; and her loopy courage once the Bentley was ditched and she'd swum and climbed and walked uncomplainingly for hours. Something very dangerous had happened over that span of time. Renita had emerged for him as an actual person. Not just a target. A human being with feelings, quirks, and plenty of attitude. He liked her. Maybe he liked her a lot.

Liking her was probably the best reason not to stick around.

He knew very well that he was poison, as toxic as the oleanders he was standing under. He couldn't possibly do her any good; all he could do was hurt and disappoint her. If he had even a shred of decency, he should run off now before he pulled her into even more disasters. But he didn't run off. He just couldn't. In his way, he was as much a captive as she was.

Plus, there were practicalities to consider. The police would soon be after him if they weren't already. For the moment he had no wheels, and heisting another car in the same town on the same night would be rash even for him. He'd been led to believe that Renita's Key West family had some wealth and influence. Maybe they'd help him out somehow or maybe he'd just con them. Or maybe he'd end up scamming Renita after all. He'd hate himself for doing it, but if the opportunity arose, he probably would. You just couldn't ask a person to go against his nature.

So he'd waited in the shadow of the oleanders. After a few long minutes, a car turned up the street. It was a rattling, boxy old sedan and in the misted glow of the streetlights it seemed to be a putrid shade of green. It was missing a hubcap and the right rear window had been replaced by plastic wrap. He hoped to hell it was not Renita's car. He did have standards, after all.

She pulled up at curbside and he climbed in.

19.

"Better to stay off the Interstate," he said, as they headed out of Old Naples and were approaching an intersection that would steer them eastward toward I-75 or on a more southerly course via old route 41, the Tamiami Trail.

"Why?" Renita asked. "You think the Saudis only patrol the superhighways?" She didn't bother trying to keep the teasing edge out of her voice. She was at the wheel, feeling much more in control now.

He didn't take the bait. "Just better," he said.

They drove in silence for a while. Strip malls gave way to gated golf communities and half-built condos fronted by cranes and epic piles of sand, until at some point the metastasizing development finally stopped spreading and they were driving through the Everglades. The moon had set by then and it was uncannily dark. Renita's high beams were misaligned and they illuminated a sort of cross-eyed tunnel through the leaning cypresses and sedges and the crucified-looking cormorants that rested in dead trees with their wings spread out to dry.

Finally, out of nowhere, Richie said, "Your parents, they

cool?"

"Compared to what? Compared to who?"

"I mean, with you bringing home a guy. They'll be okay with that? They'll put us up for a night or two?"

"Put us up, like, together? That's not happening right now, Gregory. Sorry, I mean Justin."

He let the barb pass and raised his hands to protest his innocence. Softly, even humbly, he said, "That isn't what I meant. I'm not pushing you, Renita. That's not something I would ever do. It's just that…it's just that I need a little quiet time, a little peace. I've got a few things I need to figure out."

"Yeah," she said, "I imagine you do."

Her passenger let that slide as well. Then he said, "I mean, sure, of course we'll stay in separate rooms, separate wings if you like. I mean, your parents have a big place, right?"

The question made Renita instantly regret her taunts. Here she was, teasing him, feeling righteous, trying to goad him into honesty, and meanwhile she herself had not been entirely forthright, not even close. A little sheepishly, she said, "No. Not really. It's kind of a small house."

Either Richie was surprised or he pretended to be. "Gee, the way you made it sound—"

"Maybe I exaggerated," she said. "You know, a little."

The con man smiled at that. It gave him the very rare opportunity to seize the moral high ground. "Exaggerated. Hm. Interesting. So your family, they're--?"

"Sort of average," she reluctantly admitted. "You know, working people."

"Working people," he echoed. "Regular folks. But with political connections."

This last was unmistakably payback for her digs, and Renita wrestled with the question of how much ground to yield. "Yeah, up to a point," she said at last. "They have connections locally."

Savoring the conversation now, Richie said, "Locally. Okay. But I think it's fair to say you exaggerated that as well. I think it's fair to say that a lot of what you put out there is bullshit."

With the ready indignation of someone caught at something, she said, "It's not bullshit! How can you even compare--?"

"Who's comparing?" he countered. "I'm not comparing anything. I'm just saying exaggeration, bullshit—you think there's an exact line between the two? Show me where the line is."

His tone as he said this wasn't blaming, but playful, collegial, almost Socratic. He lifted a mischievous eyebrow and half-winked, the way you wink at someone who's in on a private joke. Renita wasn't sure it was a joke she wanted to be in on. She kept silent for some moments.

They'd reached the outskirts of Homestead by then. At roadside there were little locked-up huts that, in daylight hours, would be offering freshly picked tomatoes and papayas just off the trees.

Finally the con man went on as if thinking out loud. "Hey, what's the harm? Exaggerating, bullshitting. Human nature, right? People, when they hear stuff, when they filter it, they sort of factor it in. I mean, they make allowances for a certain amount of bullshit. Don't you think?"

20.

They crossed Seven Mile Bridge at daybreak, just as the seam of the horizon was becoming visible and the sky was beginning to lift up from the sea. The highway was nearly empty and the rising sun burned like a comet in the rearview mirror as they cruised past Bahia Honda, Big Pine, Sugarloaf.

At Stock Island, just one coral outcrop before Key West, Renita suddenly pulled off the road into the gravel parking lot of a dingy old cinder-block convenience store. Ancient neon beer signs buzzed and flickered weakly in its windows; a giant Dr. Pepper bottle-cap was nailed to its front door. Equally archaic, there was a pay phone in a cracked glass booth at a corner of the building.

Renita opened the Nissan's center console and fished around in the bottom of it for some change. She said, "I need to call my folks, at least. Can't just show up with a man at seven in the morning."

She got out of the car. Richie Pestucci switched on the radio. There was a lot of static. An announcer was just finishing her dreary roundup of world news and moving on to local.

Renita tried to close the phone booth door behind her but it was frozen by rust on its sagging hinges. She dropped some coins into slots and dialed her parents' number. She knew they'd be awake, as her father's shift at Sewer Maintenance started early. Still, she expected they'd be a while answering, probably logy as usual from too much alcohol the night before. To her surprise her mother picked up on the first ring and said an alert and even exigent hello.

"Hello, Mom."

The woman at the other end of the line burst immediately into loud and extravagant tears.

In the car, the news announcer was just getting to an item about a bizarre theft and chase in Naples, after which a Bentley convertible valued at well over a quarter-million dollars was found sunk in a canal. Police were looking for suspects in a green 2004 Nissan with the Florida tag CBJ-9188.

Renita's mother said tearfully, "You're okay? You sure you're okay?"

"I'm okay, Mom. Why're you crying?"

"The police called. Three a.m.—"

"Police?"

"What happened, honey? What did you do?"

"Do? I didn't do anything. I finally went out on a date."

"You're in bad trouble, aren't you, Renita?"

"Am I? I really don't know. I don't know anything right now. Pretty crazy night. I need to come visit, talk to you and Dad and Uncle Ralph, stay a day or two. Is that okay? I'm just a couple minutes away."

"Of course. Of course it is."

"I have a friend with me."

"A friend?" Even through lingering sobs, the voice immediately hardened. "A car thief, maybe?"

"Mom, it's way more complicated than that. I'll explain, okay? I gotta go for now."

She backed out of the phone booth. Somewhere a long way north on U.S. 1, a random police siren was screaming. Renita could vaguely remember a more innocent time when police sirens didn't rattle her, when she barely noticed them. That already seemed a long while ago.

She opened the driver's side door. Even before she'd managed to sit down, Richie said, "We have to lose the car."

"What?"

"Just heard it on the radio. The police have the description, the tag, everything. Must've traced it from your license. They're after us."

Renita took a moment to absorb this. The patent unfairness of it made her feisty. "Us? Listen, pal, I'm sorry, but they're not after *us.* They're after you. They're not after me."

His voice very level, almost cooing, he said, "Are you sure of that, Renita?"

Her own voice sounded suddenly shrill in her ears. "I haven't done anything wrong!"

"I know you haven't," he said soothingly but not without a hint of condescension. "Believe me, I know. But there are other ways of looking at it. Some people might say you aided and abetted grand theft auto. Some people might say you're an accessory after the fact."

This struck her as both preposterous and terrifying. The sheer injustice of it brought a hot tear of frustration to the corner of her eye. "Accessory? Shit! So now I'm an accessory? I should have just left you stranded in Naples. I should have just left you standing there and driven away. Or even called the cops myself."

The con man didn't disagree. "You know what? You're right. You should have. But you didn't. That was probably a mistake."

Having it pointed out to her so coolly, so matter-of-factly, was so exasperating that she punched the steering wheel. "Goddamn it, Gregory or Justin or whatever the hell your name is, why didn't you just come out and admit you stole the car?"

At that, he sighed, he squirmed, embarrassment finally put a crack in his infuriating calm. He said, "Because I didn't mean to steal it."

"Didn't mean to? You stole a car by accident?"

"All I meant to do was borrow it. Borrow it and give it back before it was missed."

"It wasn't yours to borrow," she pointed out.

Ignoring that, he said, "All I had to do was bring it back on time. I bring it back on time, none of this happens. But I didn't. Why? Because we stayed out on the pier too long. Because we played kissy-face. Because you wanted to see my family's house."

"Which, by the way, does not exist," she hissed.

"Right," he countered. "I *exaggerated* about the house."

"You didn't exaggerate. You lied. And now you're saying it's my fault you stole the car?"

"That's not what I'm saying. I'm saying it's my fault, okay? It's all my fault. Does that make you feel any better?"

It didn't.

"But listen," he went on, "can I tell you, at least, why I borrowed the car to begin with?"

He tried to grab her gaze as he said this. But she was looking down at her hands, up at the dashboard, through the windshield smeared with annihilated bugs, at anything but him. She said, "I don't know why you did it and I don't care. You're a car thief and a liar and I don't care what you do or why you do it."

Undaunted, he said, "I did it to impress you. I did it because I'm so damn insecure. Your online stuff—okay, maybe it was exaggerated—but you just came across as so classy, so sophisticated. Me, I'm just a valet parker. That's right. Gregory. Like on the polo shirt. That's my real name. Gregory Hurley. No hyphens, nothing fancy. I didn't believe you'd be interested in me just for myself. So I tried to make a big first impression. Pretending to be rich, important. It was stupid. Pathetic, even. I see that now. But all along, you know what I was hoping?"

She said, "I don't care what you were hoping." But as she said it, she made the mistake of turning her head and letting her eyes drift over toward his. His eyes had lightly misted over with what might have been genuine emotion and were webby with red veins at the corners. And she was reminded how much she liked his face. She couldn't help it, she just did.

"What I was hoping," he said, "was that you'd like me a little bit, enough so I could show you who I really am. Remember what the plan was? Remember what we were going to do today?"

She remembered. Remembering broke her heart a little bit and she wouldn't say the words.

"We were going to ride bikes," he went on. "Ride bikes all day long. Like kids. Get to know each other. Talk, laugh, tell each other secrets. Wasn't that the plan?"

She bit her lip and said, "Come on, don't start with the romantic stuff. It really isn't fair."

"Maybe it isn't," he admitted. "But who started the romantic stuff? You did, Renita. That little kiss, leaning against me as we walked, touching my shoulder. It was wonderful. It was amazing. Caught me totally off guard. And I lost track of the time."

He reached out very gently and took her hand. She pulled her fingers away and he didn't try to stop her.

"I screwed up," he went on. "Big time. I admit it. But I'm not a criminal. I've never been in a mess like this before. And the fact is, we're both in trouble. We're fugitives together. We get caught, we're going to jail."

"But I haven't—"

"I know, I know," he interrupted. "But here's how a prosecutor's going to see it. I stole a car. You helped me get away. End of story. No one's going to believe I meant to give the car back. No one's going to believe you didn't know it was stolen."

Rather woodenly, she said, "But I *didn't* know." Even in her own ears the statement seemed to lack conviction.

"Maybe at the start you didn't know," he said. "But after the sirens? After we drove into the water? That's going to be a tough sell, Renita."

She bit her lip and tried to think. Suddenly she was exhausted, overwhelmed, very tired of arguing, no longer even sure she was on the right side of the arguments. Her eyes itched from the harsh glare of the morning and the rising metallic heat inside the car. Over the past few minutes things had started moving way too fast and seemed to be heading to places—courtrooms, prison—that she had never visited even in her mind. She was scared, she was confused, she felt overmatched by life. She heard herself say, "I just want to go home."

Richie Pestucci frowned and shook his head. "Not a good idea."

"My parents' house, it's only like half a mile away."

"And you don't think the cops know that? We can't go there, Renita. Think about it. Your parents harbor us, they're in trouble, too. Not fair to pull them in. Look, we can't go to your parents' and we can't keep sitting in this car."

She lightly drummed her fingers on the steering wheel and drew in a long slow breath that stretched her ribs and squared her shoulders. The gulp of air refreshed her a bit and, along with the saving resilience of youth, helped her spirits firm again, stiffened her stance of improvised but durable determination. "So what do you suggest we do? Drive it into the ocean? We've tried that, remember? Not a good long-term solution."

"Did I say anything about driving it into the ocean? Listen, I can make this right, get you off the hook at least, if not myself. I just need a little time to think. We need to just hide out for a day or so."

"Hide out?" she echoed. The phrase struck her as completely

archaic, weirdly quaint; it conjured images of desperados crouched behind barn doors or bank robbers holed up in the back room of a saloon.

"You must know someplace, Renita. You grew up here, right? There's gotta be someplace we can hide the car, hide ourselves. It's really our best chance for now."

21.

Down on Duval Street, in a noisy bacon-smelling place called Carmen's Southernmost Café, two large men and a small one were having breakfast together. The two large men were discussing the relative merits of waffles and pancakes.

One of the large men, nicknamed Soup for his custom of breaking people's jaws and knocking out their teeth and thereby putting them, if they survived at all, on liquid diets for long periods of time, was saying, "Wit' waffles, here's what I love. They got these little compartments, so you know exactly how much syrup to put on. The compartment fills up to the top, ya got the right amount. It's like, whaddyacallit, automatic. Tidy." As if to demonstrate, he pressed down the tab of the syrup dispenser with a thumb as thick as a salami and almost daintily drenched his waffle square by square.

His fellow-assassin Bats, whose specialty was smashing knees and skulls with a Louisville Slugger, was more of a pancake man. "Waffles," he said, "that's exactly the problem. Ya put stuff *on* 'em. Pancakes, stuff comes *in* 'em. Like these. Banana-Walnut. Stuff's inside. Every bite's different, a surprise, like fucking Christmas. Is there gonna be a crunch? Is there gonna be a smush? Way more interesting. Gimme pancakes any day."

The third man, the small one, stayed out of the conversation and, instead, was looking at a newspaper. The paper hid him except for the top of his head, where his dull brown hair had thinned to a downy fuzz like the coating on the backside of a baby bird. Amid his companions' clanking of utensils and slurping of coffee, he was broodingly silent until he suddenly snapped and folded back the paper so that it shrank down to a quarter of its size and was open to page three. He laid it on the table and said, "Finally a fucking break. Maybe at least."

He pointed to a brief item halfway through the crime roundup, then sat back so his goombahs could read it. It took them quite a while. Soup ran a finger along the type and underlined words with a manicured nail. Bats' lips twitched as he read. Finally Soup said, "White guy, five-eleven, athletic. Could be our guy. Won't be too fucking athletic when we're done with him."

Bats said, "But what's with the super-Waspy name, this Sanderson-something. Doesn't go with the Russian accent."

Bitterly, the small man said, "Fuck the Russian accent. The Russian accent was phony as shit. Can't believe I fell for it."

A quick and secret glance passed between the two large men. They weren't in the least surprised that Marco had fallen for the accent or the come-on or the whole cockamamie scam. That was Marco; a fast reader but he lacked for common sense. In fairness, it can't have been easy being Funzi Albertini's favorite nephew, heir apparent to the most murderous crew in Queens, and kind of a weakling shrimp in terms of his own physique. Big shoes to fill, small feet to fill them with. He tried to compensate not only by being hyper-tough and vengeful, but by imagining that, since he was clever enough to have Funzi for an uncle, that must mean he was really pretty smart and that everybody else was really pretty dumb. This made him think he'd always find an edge, an angle;

that cockiness, in turn, led to bad decisions, big mistakes. Typical he'd jump at the chance to buy a strip club at a fire sale price from some poor schnook in trouble; typical that he'd then have to beat and torture and kill the guy to erase the bitter taste of his blunder.

Soup was looking at the newspaper again, searching for the address at the bottom of the item. "1819 Jamaica Drive," he said. "Where the fuck is that?"

By reflex, Marco reached into a pocket for his phone so he could map the place. Then he remembered that the phone wasn't there because it had been in the car that was stolen by the guy who conned him, and for the about the hundredth time in the last several days he flushed with anger and humiliation.

Bats, meanwhile, had taken out his own phone and said, "Up at the north end of the island. Sort of tucked behind the airport. By a river or canal or some shit."

Marco picked up a paper napkin and thoroughly wiped his lips on it, which was odd because he'd breakfasted only on coffee and dry toast and his were the only lips at the table that weren't sticky all over with syrup. Suddenly impatient, he slid his chair back so that the legs clicked and scratched over the small tiles of the restaurant floor. "Let's go have a look," he said. "We're not gonna get this bastard sitting on our asses eating pancakes."

22.

Crossing the Cow Key Bridge was probably the hardest thing Renita had ever done. It was just a puny little span, the last link in the leapfrogging road that led at last to Key West, and the channel it crossed was hardly wider than a drainage ditch. But it was anguishing to cross because at the end of it there would be a stark choice to be made.

She could defy the so-called Gregory and turn left, toward her parents' house; or she could turn right, toward a place she'd thought of where she and her fellow fugitive could hide--and, by hiding, further embrace a misadventure in which, whether by intention or just weird circumstance, the two of them were standing together, if not exactly as allies, then as a makeshift duo against the world.

Turning left would be so much easier, so much safer.

Turning left would be, in a way, like being a kid again, or still, running back to Mom and Dad with dirty laundry, with problems that hadn't gotten solved, and doing this even in the full awareness that Mom and Dad weren't really so hot as parents. Sure, they'd be on her side. They'd hire a lawyer, probably find a way to get her off easy, maybe even scot-free. But she would have gone limping home a mess, a screw-up, maybe even an accidental felon, her big dreams of triumphing in the wider world suddenly shrunk down to the size of her girlhood bedroom.

If she went home as a flop who couldn't find her own way out of trouble, would she ever have the nerve, the confidence, to leave again? *Really* leave, really break away, really seize her independence? In a yucky sort of way, it would be pretty tempting to stay right where she was, with a house to live in, family all around, a job with the County any time she wanted one...

And, meanwhile, what would become of the handsome, lying, infuriating, devilishly persuasive Gregory? Her father would call the cops down on him in a heartbeat, of that she had no doubt. He'd be arrested, booked, easily convicted of grand theft auto, and sent off to prison in an orange jump-suit. Which was probably just what he deserved...Except maybe there was some small chance that it *wasn't* what he deserved.

He really hadn't meant to steal the car; that much she believed. He'd just borrowed it for a joy-ride to impress her. Which was wrong; but wrong enough to go to jail about? Wrong enough to wreck somebody's life about? Plus, she couldn't deny that he'd kept trying to bring her back to her hotel and she'd kept urging him to let the evening go on a little longer.

Why did he let that happen? The sweetly aching thought kept coming back to Renita that he let it happen because, in his own way, he'd been as swept up in the thrill of the moment as she was. That what started as a dumb piece of mischief became a serious crime because maybe he was falling in love a little bit. And if that was true, even if it only *might* be true, could she really abandon and betray him now? Could she watch him being dragged away in handcuffs without at least giving him a chance to fix things up?

She bit her lip, held her breath, and turned right.

23.

Bert the Shirt didn't drive much anymore, so when he did he made it an occasion. He had special clothes he liked to wear: thin calfskin gloves with open backs and snaps at the wrist, a natty glen-plaid snap-brim cap, and a racing-green silk shirt with an overall pattern of checkered flags.

Ned Preston, though antsy to get started, watched with some fascination as his host got into his regalia, and finally said, "Um, Bert, how far we going?"

"Few blocks."

"Seems like a lot of preparation for a short trip."

The old man was looking in the mirror as he adjusted the angle of his hat. "What's the length of the trip got to do with it?" he said. "Kentucky Derby's a lousy ten furlongs. Doesn't mean people don't dress for it. Now I gotta dress the dog."

"The dog?"

"Yeah, the dog. Ya don't think he's got a driving outfit? Come'ere, Nacho."

He bent low to scoop up the tiny animal then reached into the top drawer of his dresser and came out with a miniature pair of yellow-tinted goggles like the ones that 1920's racers used to wear. He carefully set these in place over the chihuahua's bulging eyes, then produced a little glen-plaid cap that matched his own except that triangular slits had been cut into the top for the dog's big ears to poke through.

Finally, they went down to the garage.

Bert's car was a 1972 Eldorado, white with a red leather interior. It had once been a convertible, but the mechanism that raised and lowered the top had long ago irreparably jammed at a point where the top was about two-thirds of the way down. So the vehicle somewhat resembled one of those old-fashioned baby carriages with an adjustable roof to shade the baby. The tires were crumbling from lack of use, flakes of dry rot curling from the wide white sidewalls.

Bert took some time repositioning his mirrors, poring over the dashboard like a test pilot checking out his instruments. When he finally started the car, the engine gave a loud clank and belched forth a puff of stale blue smoke. He inched out of his parking space, crawled toward the exit, nosed onto A1A with the infinite caution of a groundhog sniffing the air before emerging from its hole.

Eventually he hung a right onto Bertha Street, another onto Flagler, and a third onto Venetian Drive, which took them into the isolated little neighborhood where 1819 Jamaica would be found.

The precinct wasn't dreary, exactly. It was utilitarian. It seemed to be occupied by realists who had made their peace with the excoriating sunshine and corrosive salt winds of South Florida. Unlike the romantics of Old Town, who painted and repainted their wood-frame houses and gingerbread trim, who spent thousands tenting for termites and thousands more on elegant landscaping that turned jungly and anarchic every rainy season, people in this part of town kept things simple. Houses were made of cinder block. Shutters were meant to shut, not decorate. Fences were chain-link, lawns as likely as not to be Astro-turf. Clusters of scabby and enduring crotons sufficed for shrubbery, and where there were swimming pools, they tended to be above-ground models less likely to vanish someday into sinkholes.

Bert paused to reconnoiter at the empty intersection of Venetian and Jamaica. At 1819 there seemed to be a party going on. Or perhaps a vigil. In any case, there were a number of vehicles in front of and around the squat and featureless house. In the driveway there was a truck emblazoned with the seal of the Key West Sewer Maintenance department. Next to it was an old Buick Skylark whose vinyl roof had baked as hard and craggy as overcooked meringue. Parked curbside were a pickup from the Monroe County Mosquito Control Board and one of those square but righteous little cars that could run on batteries or donut grease or almost anything.

And across the narrow roadway, nestled in a pool of shade that was shrinking by the moment, was a hulking, charcoal-gray Lincoln with darkly tinted windows.

Ned Preston gestured toward it with his chin. "Shit," he said. "That's their car."

Bert kept his foot on the brake and lingered just shy of the corner. "Ya sure?"

"Can't be sure. But how many Town Cars you see down here? Goddamn thing is wider than the streets."

"Roomy trunk," Bert observed. "Handy sometimes." He hesitated for a moment while he adjusted the chihuahua's goggles and cap. Then, reaching a decision, he said, "I think ya better get inna back."

"The back?"

"Climb over. They haven't seen us yet. G'ahead, climb over. I got a whaddyacallit, a tarp kinda thing back there. Get onna floor, cover up. I'll hang out, see what I can see."

Ned said, "Bert, hey, I don't love this whole arrangement. Not fair dragging you farther into this."

"Dragging me? I didn't notice you were dragging me. Come on, before they see us. Inna back."

The con man's brother dropped his protest, and with the taken-for-granted suppleness of youth clambered over his bucket seat and settled down onto the floor. Bert parked in front of a fire hydrant and kept watch on the blank house in the morning sun.

24.

Renita's right turn put the fugitives onto the part of U.S. 1 known as Roosevelt Boulevard, a bland and dispiriting strip where chain motels and franchise restaurants had mostly squeezed out the local turquoise-painted dumps and crumbling Deco dives that had previously lined the roadway and looked out to the Gulf. Not till they were past the Publix and the Home Depot and the Denny's did Key West start looking like Key West. Then the buildings stopped matching, parking lots lost their bossy stripes. Signs had letters missing, spelling mangled, apostrophes misplaced. Liquor stores and sex shops were open bright and early.

The old Nissan pulled off the highway onto a small and frond-choked street called Hilton Haven Drive. No one knew for sure if the name was a developer's grandiose fib or some old local's joke. There was no Hilton on the street, and it wasn't much of a haven, although a few nicer homes had recently been shimmed in among the older bungalows and shacks and trailers. But Hilton Haven was basically just a gnarled finger of land that stuck out into the wrong end of Garrison Bight—the end where mangroves fouled the shoreline, and drifting sediments mysteriously moved the shoals around, and the pilings of old wooden docks were gradually hollowed out like osteoporotic bones until they could no longer hold themselves upright but leaned at defeated angles toward the sea.

The road twisted on for maybe a third of a mile, and very near the end of it Renita stopped in front of what appeared to be a vacant lot that was wildly overgrown with weeds and vagrant shrubbery and vines that curtained over the canopies of spindly, struggling trees. She turned to her companion and said, "See anything? See any way through there?"

The con man squinted at the seemingly impenetrable foliage and shook his head.

"Good," said Renita. "I do. I used to come here to play when I was a kid. Or to hide. If I was sad, or mad at my Mom or something. Seems kind of funny now. Coming back here to hide again, I mean."

She inched the car forward, and from a certain precise angle she could see a slot, a narrow apse that arched up through the jungle. She drove toward it very slowly, the Nissan's bad springs creaking and groaning over hummocks and random chunks of coral rock. Then suddenly the car was engulfed in a kind of grainy twilight as the foliage rose up on all sides, drinking up the sun and giving back the damp sweet smells of sap and decomposing leaves.

Renita switched off the ignition. She climbed out of the car, her companion following close behind. Not more than twenty yards ahead, the green tunnel gave onto bright sunlight once more. A zagging line of white stones defined a pathway through a patch of muck, and beyond it there was a ruined dock whose warped and spongy boards were here and there disconnected like the keys of a broken xylophone. Tied up to the shambles of the dock was an ancient trawler whose pilot house window was all but opaque with guano and dust and whose rusty hull was covered with slime and desiccated kelp that stretched up high above the waterline. The trawler didn't seem to be afloat. It listed at a restful angle like a fat man in a recliner.

"Used to be my grandfather's," Renita said. "When he died, there was a big fight in the family about who should get it. They fought till it wasn't worth having anymore, so it's just been sitting here as long as I can remember. My grandpa was the only person who knew I used to come here. Him, and my Uncle Ralphie. I made them promise they would never tell my parents. This is the place where no one could bother me."

Richie Pestucci nodded but he was only half-listening. In accordance with the stubborn instincts of his profession, he was already wondering how he could possibly turn this new situation to advantage or, at the very least, escape from it. He couldn't hide out on that tub of a boat for very long; that much was clear to him at once. He couldn't steal Renita's car, since it was already being searched for. Of course, if he slipped out, alone, back to the highway, there'd be plenty of other cars to steal, rides to hitch...

Lost in his own thoughts, he didn't follow the segue that led Renita to say, "And my Grandpa and me, we decided that there would be just one rule here."

"Hm?"

"In this place. On the boat. Just one rule."

"So what's the rule?"

"That anyone who comes here has to tell the truth."

Richie gave a contemptuous or perhaps just nervous little laugh. "I think they got that rule other places, too. Courtrooms. Congress. Confession booth. I don't think people really stick to it."

Softly but immovably, Renita said, "Here, we do. It's part of the fun. Think you can do it, Gregory? Think you can maybe, just possibly, tell the truth while we're here?"

25.

Inside the house at 1819 Jamaica, Pete Amsterdam was trying, however reluctantly, to act like a detective but he wasn't getting very far because Renita's relatives were acting like a family, getting sidetracked, picking petty quarrels, trying to exorcise private guilt by voicing it as public blame. He'd started with what he'd thought was a pretty safe and simple question: How long had it been, before this morning, that is, since Renita's mother had spoken with her daughter?

Carina Daughtry seemed to take the entirely neutral query as some sort of attack. She was one of those women who'd been quite attractive, a certain kind of knockout even, when she was very young and who truly didn't seem to realize that she wasn't anymore. She was only in her middle forties; she still got her hair and nails done every week, but she'd gotten sloppy, and the proof of her sloppiness was that she herself failed to notice it. Eye make-up was misapplied; lipstick sometimes stained her teeth. Her blouses weren't always buttoned right, and her thickening middle tortured the waistbands of her too-tight slacks. She stared at Amsterdam as though he'd asked her something very gauche and said, "I don't know. Two weeks. Three weeks, maybe. She doesn't call us much. She calls *him*."

She pointed at Ralphie as she said this, managing to inject decades of resentment into the small gesture and the single syllable. For the moment Renita's uncle let it pass.

"That's right," she went on. "Him she calls. Me, her mother, she doesn't call. Weeks at a time."

Renita's father spoke up then. In some ways he closely resembled his older brother Ralph—the same broad shoulders, the same loose-limbed largeness in how he moved. In other ways they were opposites, or maybe like the same person turned inside out. With Ralphie you knew just where you stood. His heart wasn't just on his sleeve, it bled on everybody else's sleeve, too. His brother Clyde kept a lot of things inside and always had. In a soft but acidic tone, he said to his wife, "You could've called her a little more often, too."

The mother was firing back even before he'd finished speaking. "And you? You don't know how to use a phone?"

Pete Amsterdam said, "Look, I was only asking—"

Clyde said, "I never did see why she had to go so far away to school. Perfectly good CC right here in town."

As ever, Ralphie came to his niece's defense. "Look, Clyde, she wanted some freedom, some opportunities. She's entitled to her own life."

"Right. And a great job she's doing of running it. Car thieves. Cop calls in the middle of the night."

Renita's uncle said to his brother, "And you? You never made any mistakes when you were young."

He threw a low-angle glance over at his wife. "I sure made one."

"You bastard!" she said. "You want to talk about mistakes? I'm the one who made the big fat mistake. Never should've gotten married so young."

"Come on, Carina. You couldn't wait to get away from that nuthouse you grew up in."

"Way too young to marry. Way too young to have a kid. So now it's all about her. Entitled to her own life. Well, of course she is. Everybody is. Everybody except me, I guess. Me, I'm just supposed to sacrifice, disappear, get kicked aside." For some reason she turned her scattershot fury back to Ralphie once again. "And now you bring this stranger to my house and in my own breakfast nook he tells me I'm a lousy mother."

"He hasn't told you anything," Ralphie pointed out. "You haven't let him talk."

Amsterdam raised his hands in a peacemaking gesture. "Look, how about we just start over? I was just trying to get a read on her mood, see if anybody sensed that maybe there was trouble coming. But let's talk about now. Early this morning you get a call from the police in Naples—"

"Three a.m.," said Clyde. "Sound asleep. Ignored the ringing at first. Figured it's some drunk wrong number. Kept ringing and ringing. Finally I answered it."

"*I* answered it," his wife corrected bitterly. "You were still boozed up, groggy—"

Amsterdam broke in before this next argument could gather much momentum. "And then, just a little while ago, you heard from Renita herself. Is that correct?"

At that, without warning or prelude, her mother exploded into sobs. There was nothing gradual about how it happened, no first soft whimper or shy little sniffle. It was a dam-burst, seismic, pure. All at once her shoulders were quaking, her skin flushed scarlet, rivers of tears carried a sediment of mascara and eye-shadow down onto her cheeks. "I was so scared," she managed. "I thought she was dead. I really did. When the phone rang again I started shaking. I thought it would be the cops calling back to say she was dead."

She stopped talking, stopped sobbing, just wept silently. Her husband, wide shoulders softly slouching, moved close to her and put his arm around her. She buried her wet face in his shirt and nestled deep against his chest. Amsterdam looked down at the floor and wondered how many times this man and woman had played out variations on this scene, being beastly to each other until just enough misery had been inflicted and they could get back to being friends.

After a pause, the detective said gently, "But it wasn't the police. It was Renita. How did she sound? What did she say?"

Composing herself, rubbing her swollen cheeks, Carina said, "Sound? I don't know. It's hard to say. I mean, the words were normal, regular. But she sounded sort of...sort of almost in a trance. Sounded like herself but not like herself. She said someone else was with her."

"She say who that someone was?"

"I kind of snapped at her," her mother admitted. "Asked if it was the car thief."

"And she said?"

"She didn't deny it. Not exactly. Just said that it was complicated."

"She say where she was calling from?"

"That's the weird part, the part that has me scared all over again. She said she was just a couple minutes from here. That she was on her way. That was, what, almost an hour ago."

"Carina, this is very important," said Amsterdam. "Are you sure that's what she said. Couple of minutes?"

She racked her frazzled brain and was embarrassed that she wasn't in fact quite sure of her daughter's exact words. "Couple of minutes. Few minutes. Something like that. But really close."

Ralphie said, "They're driving down from the mainland, it's probably Stock Island."

"Unless," said Clyde, "they'd already turned off onto Flagler."

"But Flagler...There'd probably need to be a pay phone she could've used. I mean, their cell phones would've died in the salt water, right? And Renita's was found with her purse, remember?"

Ralphie wasn't trying to offend his brother but Clyde apparently felt that he'd been dissed. "Yeah, Ralphie, I remember. It's my daughter. Remember?"

Renita's uncle seemed about to answer, but decided that the last word was not worth having.

Pete Amsterdam decided he'd had about enough of the Daughtry family for one morning and had begun to plot an escape route from the breakfast nook. Suddenly it seemed like there too many bodies and way too many festering grievances squeezed into way too tight a space. He didn't do a flying bolt, exactly, but he dipped a shoulder, aimed between a kitchen counter and a hanging rack of frying pans, and made resolutely for the door. When he was halfway through it, he said, "Call me if you hear anything more."

To his retreating back, Renita's mother said softly, apologetically, "We surely do appreciate your help."

26.

"So," Renita repeated, once they'd picked their way along the treacherously swaying dock and climbed aboard the creaking trawler, "you think you can do it? You think you can tell the truth?"

Richie sat down in a small pool of shade thrown by the pilot house. The structure's streaked and bubbled paint was lumpy against his back. He drew his knees up, hooked his elbows over them, and said, "Maybe."

The prevaricating word did not strike Renita as a promising start. "Maybe?"

"Maybe," he said again. "Look, you want an honest answer, that's an honest answer. If I said yes, that wouldn't be an honest answer. Maybe you'd like it better, it would sound more definite, but it wouldn't be honest. People mix up honest with definite all the time. Two very different things. Trust me on that."

"It's a little difficult right now to trust you on anything," Renita said. She did her unconscious trick of holding his gaze just a fraction longer than was usual or comfortable.

Richie just shrugged, scratching his back against the paint.

She sat down on the deck across from him and hugged her knees, her posture inadvertently mirroring his. "Well, okay," she said, "let's give it a try at least. Let's start with something really easy. Your name. Is it really Gregory Hurley?"

"No." He said it simply and without apology.

His directness disarmed Renita and she wasn't sure if she was making progress or if it was just that her companion was changing up his tactics, using an admission of past lies as a smokescreen for current and future ones. "Fine. Good," she stammered. "Not Gregory Hurley. So what is your real name?"

"I don't have one."

"You don't have one? Come on, everybody has a real name."

"I don't. I mean, I did, but it was taken away from me. I woke up one morning and it was gone."

"Gone? Where did it go?"

The young man with the diamond-shaped face looked down at the rotting boards of the old trawler's deck. "It didn't go anywhere. It was just erased, blotted out."

"Okay," said Renita, secretly disappointed that the conversation seemed to be turning into some sort of elaborate but meaningless word game and that she was getting no closer to any reliable sense of the man she was now stranded with. "But back when you had a real name, what was it?"

"Richie. Richie Pestucci."

She didn't believe him. Why should she? It was the third different name she'd heard him call himself, plus it didn't go at all well with her impressions of him so far. *Richie* sounded far too informal, too easygoing, too happy-go-lucky. And *Pestucci*? It was just too...too *something*, too made-up sounding, like one of those semi-comic Italian names you might hear in a movie or TV show. Not bothering to hide her dubiousness, she said, "All right, Richie Pestucci. And are you really a valet parker?"

"No," he said, and in a perfectly level and everyday tone, he added, "I'm a professional impostor."

She thought he was kidding. Or at least exaggerating by a very wide margin. Playing along, she said, "Oh, and do you have many disguises?"

"I don't need disguises. Disguises are for amateurs, for Halloween."

"Okay, no disguises. So who have you pretended to be lately?"

"That's what people don't understand," he said. "I don't pretend to be somebody. I become somebody."

Her tone somewhere between teasing and patronizing, she said, "Sorry, my mistake. So who have you become lately."

"You mean before Gregory? Before Justin? Before that I became a Russian gangster who hung out at a strip club near La Guardia. Convinced some poor schmuck that I owned the building and had to flee because Putin's goons were after me. Sold him a phony deed for two hundred thousand dollars and then I drove off with his car. I hid most of the money not far from here before I skipped out and went to Naples."

"I see," said Renita, not for a moment tempted to believe it. The story, after all, was even more far-fetched, more fantastic, than the malarkey about his rich imaginary family with a Gulf-front estate in Naples. It was even miles beyond the nonsense about Special Ops and Saudi agents. Well, Renita had studied this kind of thing. Compulsive, pathological lying. A syndrome in which the only response to being caught in a lie was to tell a bigger lie, then a bigger one still, careening and spiraling ever-outward from reality until the last shreds of fact and credibility were left far behind, and the liar found himself totally unmoored, alone, a pariah in self-imposed exiled from the truth. After a moment the young woman continued, not in a tone of blame but of earnest therapeutic sympathy. "You just can't do it, can you? You just can't."

"Do what?"

"Tell the truth."

"But I am telling—"

She shook her head and raised a hand to stop him. "It's okay," she said. "If you can't, you can't. I won't press you anymore. Maybe it's better if you just don't try."

27.

Pete Amsterdam hadn't meant to let the screen door of 1819 Jamaica slam behind him, but as he barreled out of the seething little house into the heightening sunshine of the morning, it did. He winced at the ugly jangle then walked quickly across the scrubby yard and through the gate of the chain-link fence toward his square and virtuous little car, which started up without making a sound.

He was just rounding the corner when he saw, parked against the opposite curb, a vehicle he recognized at once, since there was none other like it in Key West or very possibly anywhere else: An ancient Caddy with a paralyzed ragtop and a chihuahua in racing goggles and a glen-plaid cap perched on the driver's side doorframe. Amsterdam, like practically everyone in town, knew the car's owner as a regular at the Eclipse Saloon, a fixture on Smathers Beach, and a genial though ungrammatical fellow with a knack for sticking his capacious nose into other people's business. Pulling close and rolling down his window, the detective said, "Bert, what the hell you doing here?"

The old man threw a look that Amsterdam didn't quite catch toward the Town Car parked on Jamaica Drive and partly visible through the tangled shrubbery. Then he said, "Otnay ownay."

Amsterdam said, "What?"

Bert raised his chin about an inch toward the Lincoln. "At-thay arcay."

The detective looked at the old man in his snap-brim cap that matched the dog's and said, "Jeez, Bert, I'm sorry. You had a stroke or something? I can't understand a word you're saying."

Frowning, looking slightly disappointed in Amsterdam, the old man said, "I ain't had a stroke. It's pig Latin. Ya never heard pig Latin?"

"Eighth grade maybe. Anyway, what the hell you doing here?"

Bert played it cagey. "It might be *a propos* and I think I'd be well within my rights to turn that inquiry around and on its head and ask what the hell *you're* doing here."

Tersely, Amsterdam said, "On a case."

Bert tried not to laugh. "A case? You?"

"No one's more surprised than I am," Amsterdam admitted.

"So happens I'm on a case also," Bert volunteered.

"You? Oh Christ, what the hell's it got to do with—"

"We oughtta talk. I got a guy in the back seat. Under the tarp."

"Under the tarp? Like, a body?"

"Not a body. A guy. Stick your head out, Ned."

Ned Preston did as he was asked. It had been hot and airless and smelly under the tarp. His face was sweaty and glistening, his hair dappled with dust and lint. It made for an unsavory first impression.

Amsterdam said, "What the—"

"Listen," Bert interrupted, "this is not the time and place for a summit meeting or any sort of lengthy or let's say edifying conference, okay?" He once again lifted his chin toward the Lincoln and this time the detective finally followed the gesture. "Those skull-breakers in the Town Car, eventually they're gonna turn around. What say we meet over at your house?"

🛶 🛶 🛶

Five minutes later, the three men and the dog were settled into plastic chairs in the detective's small backyard. A light midmorning breeze had come up; it made the palm fronds rustle and the shadows dance, but what riveted Bert's attention was the menagerie of small dead creatures spread around the apron of the pool. Gesturing toward them with a gnarled forefinger, he said, "What's with the frogs?"

"Had Mosquito Control out yesterday," said the detective.

"Ah," the old man said. "You got the full Chernobyl. Make sure you pick 'em up before that goo they got dries out and glues 'em to the tiles. Bastard to clean up once that happens. Skin peels off, leaves the guts."

"Good advice, Bert. Thanks. But about your little expedition this morning—"

The old man was still staring with dispassionate scientific interest at the tiny corpses shriveling in the sun. "What's that one over there?" he interrupted. "Can't quite see that far. But those little legs...Mouse?"

"Rat," said Amsterdam.

"Kills good, that stuff."

"Very good," the detective said. "I mean well. But about your showing up on Jamaica Drive. Why were you there?"

"Why were *you* there?" countered the man with the chihuahua.

"Come on, Bert, this isn't a goddamn Mafia sitdown and you're not a *consigliere* anymore. We're just sharing information here."

The old man stuck to what he saw as proper protocol. "Good. Or well if you prefer. You first."

Amsterdam allowed himself a somewhat exasperated sigh but didn't see the point of arguing. "Okay, okay," he said, and he gave his visitors a brief account of how he met Renita's uncle, and of the mosquito man's fear that his niece had gone missing, and of the terrifying phone call from the Naples cops in the middle of the night, and of the little information they had about the man who the niece was believed to be with. Wrapping up his story, the detective said, "There, that's all I got. Now show me yours."

Bert, ever the diplomat, said, "Ain't my place to show it. Ned here, it's really his story, it's really up to him how much he wants to say."

At that, Amsterdam and the young man with the diamond-shaped face and dusty hair locked eyes. It was the first time they'd looked at each other more than casually, more than politely, and it was one of those pure primate moments when males under stress take each other's measure. Were they equals? Were they threats to one another? Would they be allies? Adversaries? Without dropping the stare, without surrendering, Ned said, "The guy the niece is with, I'm almost positive it's my brother. Twin brother."

What this conveyed to Amsterdam was that the brother was, at the very least, a car thief. This did nothing good for his opinion of his visitor. Stonily, he said, "Go on."

"Go on where?"

"Like, for instance, why are they together? They met on a dating site, is that correct? Your brother use dating sites often?"

"I don't know."

"Where's he from?"

"New York."

"New York," repeated Amsterdam. "And he comes all the way to Florida for a date?"

"He was in Florida anyway," said Ned.

"Why?" the detective pressed. "Why was he in Florida?"

By this point the young man had begun to flush a beset and increasingly angry brickish red, and Bert thought it best to intervene before the sparring became a flat-out fight that might leave an irreparable grudge. He said, "Come on, Pete, you don't have to give this guy the third degree. There happens to be some things going on here that are not right on the surface or let's say readily apparent and that as of this moment you don't know shit about."

"So enlighten me," the detective said.

Bert looked to his young friend for permission to explain. Ned granted it with the smallest possible nod, and the old man, in his tangled, mangled way, filled Amsterdam in about the strip club con with its ill-advised target, and the poor decision to drive off in the mobster's vehicle, the upshot of these misjudgments being that ruthless and determined killers were now in hot pursuit.

Amsterdam took a moment to navigate Bert's grammar and digest this unexpected and unwelcome information, then turned back to Ned. "Lemme make sure I have this right. So your brother isn't just a car thief and possible sex predator. He's a con man too?"

"Hey, no need to get judgmental," Bert protested. "Everybody has to be something."

The detective ignored that. "Is he dangerous?"

Under the circumstances it was a fair and natural question but Ned found it genuinely surprising, appalling even. He'd never thought of his brother as dangerous, never let himself imagine it. Dishonest, sure. Devoid of conscience, apparently. But did he ever actually hurt anyone? Like, physically? Permanently? The possibility made Ned feel sick and hollow and for a few seconds he couldn't speak.

"Is he violent?" Amsterdam pressed.

"I don't think so," Ned managed.

"Armed?"

"I doubt it. That wouldn't be his way."

"But you can't say for sure, can you?"

"No, I can't."

"Ever seen him snap?"

That was one goading question too many, and Ned finally stood up for his brother--literally stood up, pressing down hard on the arms of his chair until his weight came clear of it and he was leaning forward over the balls of his feet. "Look, he isn't dangerous, okay? I just don't see that in him. I don't think he owns a gun. Plus, he's the one the Mob is after. *He's* the one that's in danger. Isn't that obvious?"

Leaning forward in turn, abruptly lifting his usually unaggressive chin close in to the other man's torso, Amsterdam said, "What's obvious to me is that your brother is not the good guy in this story."

There was a silence, a standoff. Even in the open air, even against the smell of flowers and the ripening stink of poisoned animals, the musk of close confrontation could be detected. Bert placidly stroked his dog and glanced back and forth between the two clenched men. Finally he said soothingly, "Okay, not the good guy maybe, but not the worst guy either. I mean, come on, Pete, we got real killers here."

Amsterdam wasn't ready to back off. "Right. And why? Because this con man fucked up and is on the run and has this young woman as a hostage."

Bert said, "Wait a second. Who says she's a hostage?"

"Who says she isn't?" the detective fired back. "Or at least couldn't be used as one in a tight spot." Turning once again to Ned, he said, "Your brother, you say he isn't violent. How do you think he'd act if he was cornered?"

"He wouldn't get cornered. He's too smart."

"Excuse me, but so far I don't see much evidence of that. How do you think he'd act?"

Feeling cornered himself, Ned Preston pushed his chair away with the backs of his knees and paced a few steps on the corpse-strewn pool apron. "How would he act? I think he'd say fuck you and fuck your questions. Look, I didn't come to your house to be browbeaten. I don't know why I came here at all. Guess 'cause for some crazy reason I imagined we'd be on the same side."

The sun had topped the trees by now. The breeze died and the shadows shrank in from the edges like evaporating puddles. The rising heat made the blood pound in people's ears and temples.

"Side?" hissed Amsterdam. "I'll tell you what side I'm on. I'm on my client's side. I'm on the side of this big lovable slob who came to me because he's worried sick about his niece who's mixed up with your con man brother. Came to me because he loves her so much, 'cause he loves her no matter what. Loves her if she's strange, loves her if she makes mistakes, loves her if she's possibly a little crazy. That's whose side I'm on, okay?"

Ned took that in as he paced, tried his damnedest to weigh it fairly, to consider without rancor the logic and the justice of it. Then he swallowed, licked his lips, and said very softly, "Okay, I get it. I really do. Guy loves his niece. Fair enough. But what about me? I'm not entitled to love my brother?"

It was the tone as much as the words that began to defuse the tension in the yard full of dead frogs. Ned had spoken only briefly yet seemed slightly winded by the effort it had cost him. Amsterdam eased out of his rigid posture and looked down at the tiles that framed the pool.

Bert stroked his dog and kept his face faultlessly neutral. After a moment he exhaled with a wheeze and said, "Well. You guys got anything more you need to get off your hairy chests? No? Then maybe we can stop arguing a couple minutes and see if somehow maybe we can work together to figure out this fucking mess."

PART THREE

28.

"Your little tell-the-truth game," said Richie Pestucci. "Maybe it's my turn to ask a few questions."

"Okay, sure," she said.

They'd moved out of the sharp glare of the sun into the dimness and relative cool of the trawler's cabin. Spiders had scuffled away when Renita shouldered open the warped sliding door; a displaced seagull had flown off of the roof, bitterly complaining.

Inside, except for the thick coating of oily dust on everything and the slight leaning of the floor, the cabin was pretty much as Renita remembered it. There were two compartments, surprisingly roomy. One held the steering wheel with its peeling varnish, an old navigation table filled with archaic paper charts, a very rudimentary galley, and a pair of blue settees with frays and tears between the fabric and the piping. The other compartment, behind a stout oak partition, featured a wide berth whose improvised mattress was unfurled between the curving walls of the hull. Renita would have loved to lie down in there a while, but she didn't. Bedrooms suggested bedroom ideas, planted bedroom expectations. No way was she ready to go there.

So she stayed discreetly in the forward compartment, flipping over a settee cushion and sitting down on the side that wasn't dusty. Richie stood next to the varnished wheel, his arm draped over it in a manner that was somehow lawyerly.

"Okay," he said. "First question. When we were up in Naples and you went to get your car, why didn't you take off? Why didn't you just get clear of me?"

"That's a hard one to start with," she complained. "Can't we sort of ease in with something easier?"

"No, we can't. So why didn't you leave?"

She was leaning forward, her hands lightly squeezing down on the edges of the cushion. She could feel crumbling foam rubber in the split that paralleled the piping; it was impossible not to pick at it a little. "Not sure," she admitted. "Maybe I just wanted to see what would happen next. Simple curiosity."

"Which often leads to trouble," he put in.

She didn't disagree, just glanced off toward the galley at a pile of beer cans so old that their brand names could no longer be read. "I guess I was having fun. Weird fun, but fun. I mean, I've been on first dates that were way less interesting. Or, who knows, maybe it's just that I like your face."

"And I like yours," he volunteered. "A lot. I think you're really beautiful."

She blushed just slightly at that and the faint reddening of her skin darkened the faint freckles and made her eyes look even greener. "You're telling the truth?"

"What's the difference? You don't believe me anyway. Next question. Are you afraid of me?"

She thought that over for a moment, but not for long. "No," she said. "I don't think I am. Not much, at least. Maybe just a tiny bit, in that woman-alone-with-a-strange-man kind of way. Not more than that. If it was more than that I would've taken off."

He nodded. There was a sudden twitching at the corner of his eye and Renita couldn't tell if he was close to tearing up or if the conversation had brought out a previously hidden nervous tic. But he just said, "Good. I'm glad you're not afraid of me."

There was a silence marred only by the scratch of birds landing on the pilot house roof and the whoosh of them taking off again.

"Some women, lot of women," he went on softly, "would be. Depending how much they knew, I guess. I have a stinking rotten past, Renita. I've been in prison twice."

The young woman did not seem scandalized or even especially surprised. "Cars?"

"Cars. Bad checks. Stolen credit cards. Identity theft."

"People make mistakes."

"Yeah, but if they make them over and over again, it's probably who they are."

"So that's really who you are?" she asked. "A criminal?"

He raked his hand along the rim of the trawler's wheel. The ancient varnish was cracked and spiky, punishingly rough to the touch. "I wish I knew for sure," he said. "It changes with every new name. I confuse myself a lot, if you want to know the truth."

"Maybe that's part of why I stayed with you," she said.

"To watch me be confused?" He lifted an eyebrow, attempted a wry smile. "You studying me for schoolwork?"

"Maybe," she admitted. "Probably that's part of it."

He looked away a moment and when his eyes turned back the smile was gone from them. "Well, it isn't schoolwork, Renita. It's me and it's you and we're in trouble and we're out here just the two of us and nobody knows where we are, and you don't know and I don't know what's going to happen next."

She wasn't aware of fear starting up until she noticed that her mouth had suddenly gone dry. "Now you're scaring me a little, Richie. Is that what you're trying to do? Are you trying to scare me now?"

"No. At least I don't think I am. Guess I'm just trying to say that sometimes it's a good thing to be a little scared. Concentrates the mind. Speeds up the reflexes. Helps you make the right decision."

She said nothing, just toyed with the crumbs of foam rubber that had broken loose from the torn and brittle cushion.

After a few seconds he went on. "I don't want to go back to prison, Renita. I'd do pretty much anything to avoid it. You need to know that. If it comes to going back to jail, I just don't know how things would play."

"Maybe it doesn't have to come to that," she said, though she herself didn't quite believe it and couldn't pinpoint the moment when she'd started taking his side. "You didn't mean to steal—"

"Doesn't matter what I meant to do," he interrupted. "Matters what happened. Matters that I have a record. Renita, listen...I like you. If I wasn't so screwed up I'd probably be in love with you by now. So here's a piece of advice. If you get another chance to break away from me, take it. Please. Don't wait around. Don't hesitate. Don't take any more chances."

29.

By the time Uncle Ralph emerged through the screen door of 1819 Jamaica Drive, the three men in the Town Car had gotten very antsy and very testy. The patch of shade they'd parked in had shrunk to nothing and become a broiler with searing sun above and softening asphalt below. Even with the A/C blasting it was hellishly hot inside the car and the heat was souring the heavy breakfasts in their stomachs. For a moment, Marco Albertini watched the big loose-limbed man in the County uniform walking slowly toward his truck, then he suddenly said to his enforcers, "Grab him."

"Grab him?" said Soup.

"Grab him!" said Marco, more emphatically. He was suddenly mad at the guy with the Mosquito Control truck, like it was all his fault that they were sweating bullets, getting heartburn, and accomplishing nothing. "All fucking morning we're sitting here," he said. "Our guy never shows, the girlfriend never shows, we coulda just as well stayed drinking coffee. Let's get some goddamn information, at least."

The enforcers glanced at each other across the console, then, with a practiced if not exactly graceful synchrony, sprang out of the car. They didn't have to run to overtake Ralphie. In fact, when he was still a few steps from his truck, he stopped and turned to face them. His first vague thought, before he'd heard them speak or looked at them very closely, was that they were probably reporters, gossip-mongers looking for some dirt about the local girl who was mixed up with this crazy business of the sunken Bentley. Ralphie didn't want them bothering his touchy brother and his hysterical wife. He asked the two men if he could help them though there was nothing friendly in the offer.

Bats turned to Soup and said, "He wants to know if he can help us. Isn't that nice? People are nice down here, ain't they?"

Soup didn't answer. He just said to Ralphie, "Our boss wants to talk to you."

Ralphie's adrenal glands seemed to figure out before his brain did that these two large men in pointy shoes were not in fact reporters. Over the course of a second or two, his lagging mind put the pieces together and he understood these guys were thugs, mobsters, and not just any mobsters, but mobsters from New York. Partly it was their sardonic accents that triggered this unhappy conclusion; partly it was a certain intonation of the simple word *boss*. In any case, a fear that was quicker than thought had put a milky feeling at the backs of his legs and sent a ready but useless tautness into the muscles of his arms and shoulders. Trying to keep his voice steady, he said, "Talk? What about?"

Bats said, "Waste of breath, ain't it, to talk about what we're gonna talk about before we talk about it? Let's go to the car."

Ralphie didn't like that idea at all. He'd seen plenty of movies. Bad things happened once they got you in the car. Once they got you in the car, they could do whatever they wanted. He pointed to a spot where a poinciana tree was throwing an oasis of shade. "How about over there? Nice and cool."

"Inna car," Bats said again, and they started walking Ralphie over. They didn't drag him and didn't exactly push him, just coaxed him along with little knee or shoulder bumps when his reluctant feet stopped moving.

Soup yanked open the back door of the Lincoln and shoved Ralphie in. Ralphie's head clunked on the doorframe and it took him a moment to get his long limbs folded and arranged.

Marco Albertini said to him, "Close the fucking door, you're letting the A/C out." He didn't seem to notice that the A/C had no chance against the Key West sun or that the paltry ration of air inside the car stank of sweat and after-shave and half-squelched belches that contributed vapors of maple syrup. The small balding man gestured toward the house and continued, "That big pow-wow in there. What the fuck was it about?"

Ralphie, trying to stay calm, trying not to get muddled or pass out from lack of oxygen, said, "What's it to you?"

Marco had the morning newspaper in his hand. By way of answer he slapped Ralphie across the face with it. The slap didn't hurt much but it was startling and humiliating and it set the tone. "The guy who stole that car in Naples," the little boss said commandingly. "Where is he?"

"I have no idea. I don't know anything about that guy."

"Okay," said Marco, "so let's start over. And gimme a fucking answer this time. The get-together in there. What was it about?"

"It's my brother's house. Younger brother. They're worried about their daughter. My niece."

"Spare me the shit about your family tree, okay? This niece, she's with the guy that stole the car?"

"I don't know where she is. I don't know where either of them are."

"But they're together?" Marco pressed.

"Look, I really don't know. She was with him when the car got sunk."

No one had invited Soup into the conversation but he piped up anyway. "She was with that piece of shit? What is she, some kinda whore?"

Ralphie didn't remember reaching over the headrest to strangle Soup, but next thing he knew his hands were wrapped around the big man's throat, fingers pressing on his Adam's apple and clawing at his collarbone. Soup, big as he was, jerked up and down like a man in the electric chair, but the choke hold was abruptly released when Bats swiveled around and placed the muzzle of his 9 mm firmly against Ralphie's forehead.

For a moment everybody froze, as in some macabre version of green light/red light. Ralphie's death-grip lost its power though his hands stayed wrapped around Soup's neck. Bats lightened the pressure on the pistol but still held it where its muzzle had stamped a perfect circle in the skin between and slightly above Ralphie's eyes. The simian musk of men getting violent further fouled the scant air inside the Lincoln, then, as if on cue, as if in response to the rhythmic prompts of an invisible conductor, the men relaxed in unison from their rather preposterous positions and went back to sitting as before.

Quietly, as though nothing much had happened, Marco said, "So I take it you're fond of your niece."

"Very."

"That's nice. But something you have to understand is that we don't give a shit about her one way or the other. The guy she's with, him we care about. He conned me and we're gonna kill him. That part's simple. You understand?"

He said it very matter-of-factly, and Ralphie didn't see any point in answering.

"Now with your niece it's different," the balding man went on. "To us she's mainly just a complication. Furniture. She might get in the way. And the way life is, kind of random I mean, sometimes people get hurt if they're in the way."

Ralphie heard himself say, "You hurt my niece, I'll kill you."

For some odd reason that made Marco smile. He looked at his captive more closely and read the name embroidered above the pocket of his shirt. He said, "So, it's Ralphie? I like you, Ralphie. You got spirit. You're a good uncle. I have a good uncle, too. Mine's name is Funzi. Very powerful man, very wise. Taught me everything I know. One of the things he taught me is that you should never make a threat you can't make good on. Generally bounces back and bites you in the ass. So I'm gonna ignore your threat to kill me. Let's act like you never said it. But about your niece—"

Ralphie cut in but he'd pretty much used up his bravado. His tone now wasn't quite pleading but it was getting close. "Please. Don't hurt her. You said yourself—"

"That I don't give a shit about her," Marco interrupted in turn. "Which is true. But here's the thing. When we ice our guy, we can be more careful or less careful about how we do it. More careful, good chance your niece comes out of it okay. Less careful, well, shit happens. It's up to you."

"Up to me?"

"Come on, Ralphie, ain't it clear?"

To Renita's uncle nothing was clear at that moment.

"You're looking for your niece," the little gangster went on. "We're looking for the scumbag she's with. You know the territory down here. We don't. Whose chance of finding them is better? Frankly, my money's on you."

"But listen, I have no idea—"

"That's why I think you're gonna help us," Marco interrupted. "Help our chances of doing a quick and tidy job without anybody extra gets hurt."

To Bats he said, "Give this nice man your phone number. Write it down."

The big man scrawled it on a candy wrapper with a hand that seemed designed for crushing walnuts, not drawing numbers with a pencil.

"You find that fucker," the boss went on, "you call us. Anytime. Day or night. It's in your interest, Ralphie. Do it for your niece. Whaddya say?"

30.

Renita hadn't realized just how exhausted she was until she allowed herself to settle back a little deeper into the embrace of the torn blue cushions, to surrender to the lulling heat and the comfortingly familiar salty, beery smell of the trawler's cabin. Quite suddenly the long-fended-off fatigue overtook her like a kind of drunkenness, making her vision blurry at the corners, reducing all sounds to a garbled but musical background murmur. She gave in to a delicious, overwhelming yawn and let her body slump to horizontal on the old settee.

As she drifted toward sleep, she savored the awareness of being in her girlhood refuge, and once she'd dozed off, this awareness mellowed down not into a dream of peace, but peace itself. There were no thoughts, no images, no sense of time; nothing but the anchored though weightless sense of her body floating on its cushions.

This happy oblivion lasted maybe twenty minutes, then, as her doze began to lighten, she became aware once more of sounds, sounds that broke free of the general hum and gradually took on meaning. There was a sound like the sliding of a balky drawer, then like the opening and closing of cabinets on sticky hinges. There were dull soft scrapes and clangs of metal against metal. There was the soft creak of footsteps moving away. She dozed a little more.

When she woke up she seemed to be alone in the pilot

house. She blinked around to its four corners, then heard herself say, "Richie?" The silence that followed had the particular bottomless resonance of a place that was empty.

Standing up on tingling feet, she peeked rather shyly around the oak partition to the berth that held the dangerous big mattress. He wasn't on it.

Puzzled but not yet seriously worried, she stepped out onto the deck. Her eyes had not yet adjusted to the probing, ferocious sunshine and for a moment all she saw was a knifing white glare with even sharper green glints off the water. Squinting, she looked all around the trawler, then down onto the leaning snaggle-toothed dock and along the snaking row of white stones that made a pathway through the muck. She didn't see Richie in any of those places, and a feeling, muted at first, began to grow in her that Richie had fled, that Richie was gone. This should have been a relief. It *was* a relief...sort of. So why did it feel like an abandonment, a desolation?

She remembered the sounds she'd half-heard as her sleep was lightening. They must have been the sounds of Richie quietly rummaging around for things. What things? Some ancient tins of food? Cans of beer gone long since flat and rancid? Rusty knives that might pass for weapons? She remembered the soft shuffle of his retreating footsteps. In her mind, she pictured him walking out and couldn't help wondering if he'd paused at least for a last look back at her. She felt wounded and belittled that he hadn't even felt the need to say goodbye. And without a goodbye, she wasn't quite ready to believe or accept that he was gone.

Still drowsy, she went to look for him. With some of the wobbly grace of a sleepwalker, she stepped down from the trawler onto the dock and headed toward the narrow clearing where the car was hidden. She walked slowly to delay not finding him. As she walked she worked at reminding herself it was a good thing that he'd sneaked away. Best for everybody. And yet...This just wasn't how it was supposed to happen. Wasn't she the captive? It should have been her choice to escape, to bolt, not his. She'd stood by him, put herself at risk. For what? To be ditched without so much as a farewell scene? It wasn't fair and it hurt. She'd known this man for all of sixteen hours and yet his sudden absence left a hollow and an ache.

She stepped into the dim and narrow clearing. Random shafts of sunlight filtered through the foliage, revealing a floating world of dust and spores and tiny daytime insects. Her car sat silent and forlorn perhaps thirty yards away. The clearing seemed blank and empty otherwise. The young woman hadn't intended to speak aloud, but then she heard herself once again call out his name. "Richie?"

The leaves and vines drank up the sound, and no answer, not even the faintest echo, came back to her.

She said it louder. The silent response this time had something mocking in it, and Renita, at first just sad, began to feel frustrated and angry in addition. She'd done nothing to deserve this absurd but stinging sense of loss. The injustice of it made her want to cry, but instead of crying she crossed her arms in front of her and called out, just short of shouting, "God damn you, Richie!"

She heard Richie's voice innocently answer, "What?"

Then he stood up behind the old Nissan, where he'd been squatting to remove the rusted-on license plate with the tools and can of lubricant he'd scavenged from the drawers and cabinets. He was shirtless and his body gleamed with sweat.

Renita said, "I...I thought you'd left."

He mopped his forehead with the back of his hand. "You minded?"

She said nothing.

He held up the battered license plate. "Doubt anyone would have noticed it, but why take chances?" He gathered up the tools and sidled around the car. He was moving toward Renita but she had the feeling he was going to walk right past her.

Belatedly, she answered his question. "Yeah, Richie, I minded. It felt lousy. I felt cheated."

The con man, whose long habit was to cheat anyone out of anything and not to feel the slightest qualm about it, actually felt a little bad this time. Waving a screwdriver and a wrench in a sort of sheepish explanation, he just said, "Sorry I upset you."

"It's okay now," she said, holding his eyes for a disconcerting extra fraction of a beat. "It's really okay. But can we make a deal, at least? Can we promise each other that, whoever takes off first, we at least take a minute to say goodbye?"

31.

Ralphie was nauseous by the time he was released from Marco Albertini's Town Car.

He walked slowly through the fierce but cleansing sunshine toward his truck, taking deep and measured breaths along the way, struggling to get the fresh and salt-laced air past the sick lump in his solar plexus. He waited until the Lincoln had pulled out of Jamaica Drive and the queasiness had subsided, then he switched on his ignition and drove to Pete Amsterdam's house.

He arrived just as Bert and the dog and Ned were getting ready to leave, and there was an extremely awkward moment on the doorstep.

Ralphie knew Bert a little bit—everybody did—and they said a brief but cordial hello. Then Amsterdam introduced his client to Ned Preston, explaining who the young man was. That's what led to the awkward part.

Ned extended a hand; Ralphie didn't want to shake it. Maybe it was unfair to blame one family member for the actions of another, but he couldn't get past the fact that this was the twin of the con man who was endangering his niece. He fell back half a step as though Ned carried some contagion and shot him a look that was not aggressive, just frighteningly icy. Then he said in a somewhat glazed and neutral tone, "Some gangsters just recruited me to help them kill your brother. I don't see why I shouldn't do it."

Ned stared back at him, didn't look especially surprised, said nothing.

Amsterdam, wishing as he often did that he'd never taken the first small step toward involvement in other people's problems, said, "Um, maybe we should talk inside."

Settled in the living room, he said to Ralphie, "They recruited you? How?"

The mosquito man told them about being bundled into the Town Car, the contretemps with Soup, the gun pressed to his forehead, the threats and counter-threats, the promise that, one way or another, the con man would be taken out.

Bert was shaking his head. "Flat-out murderers, these guys. Assassins. They oughta be in Sing-Sing."

The chihuahua mistakenly took its cue from that and launched into its one and only trick. *Ow-ow-OWWW! Ow-ow-OWWW!*

"Not now, Nacho. Not now."

When the howling had died down and the dog was drowsing again in Bert's lap, Amsterdam said, "Ralphie, listen, I know you're all worked up, I know you've been through a lot, but think about it. What they're asking you to do, it's not some little favor. It's extremely serious business. Like twenty years in the slammer business. They're asking you to aid and abet a murder."

Grudgingly, blandly, Renita's uncle said, "I guess you could look at it that way."

Ned Preston could no longer keep silent. He was pinching the arms of his chair but his voice sounded like it was his own throat that was being squeezed. "How the fuck else can you look at it? They want you to lead them to a guy they want to kill. A guy you know they want to kill. A guy they've *told* you they want to kill.

How the fuck else can you look at it?"

Ralphie had no ready answer for that. He just stared at Ned. Ned stared back. The stares seemed to generate mysterious, invisible waves that created an illusion of the living room walls bellying out, the windows being distorted from their rectangular shapes. Both men began unconsciously to ball their fists. The odd thing was that there was no personal animosity between the two of them, none at all. No history, no grudges. Both decent and well-meaning guys. Yet for the moment they were ferocious enemies simply because of who they were related to. It made no sense. It was utterly perverse and entirely human.

When the stare had used up most of its wattage, Bert the Shirt said softly to Ralphie, "Excuse me, but can we please back up a step? These murderers that want your help. I presume and also would imagine that they're offering something in return. An incentive or what might called a *quid pro quo.* In other words, a deal."

"Yeah, of course they are. I call them up—"

"Call them up?" Amsterdam cut in.

"Yeah, they gave me a number, told me call anytime. Deal is, I help them find their guy, they pretty much promise not to hurt my niece."

"Pretty much promise," Bert echoed. The dubious words hung in the air while he petted his dog then plucked a dog hair off of his driving shirt with the pattern of checkered flags. Finally he went on, "And you believe them?"

The question was very gently asked but, even so, it made Ralphie's face sag. It wasn't that Bert's words had planted a seed of doubt; the seed of doubt had already been there, but, caught in one of the thousand gray areas between believing and not-believing, Ralphie had been trying to ignore it. Now that the skepticism had been spoken aloud, he couldn't do that anymore. Sorrowfully, he said, "I really don't know."

Trying to be tactful or at least no more graphic than was absolutely necessary, Bert said, "Guys like this, at moments of stress they have a way of forgetting what they promised. And they really don't like witnesses. You understand that, right?"

Renita's uncle was pretty drained by then. He could barely even nod. His hands, no longer fists, hung limp from his wrists and he looked straight down between his knees at the wooden floor.

Amsterdam said, "So I think where we're going with this is that our best shot of saving Renita is by bailing out the con man too. May not be fair. Not saying the guy deserves to be bailed out. But it seems like the best or only way. We gotta try for both. Agreed?"

He looked at Ralphie. A spasm of distaste riffled the big man's features like a puff of wind on water, and even when it had passed he did not seem totally resigned. He said nothing, promised nothing. He just glanced at Ned from underneath an eyebrow. Ned looked back with slightly less resentment than had been there before. It was a modest, sour, and tentative truce but it was as far as the two of them would go.

Trying to sound upbeat, like he'd just pulled off some major diplomatic coup, Amsterdam said, "All right, then. So let's pool what we know about where these two might be."

Discouragingly, Bert said, "Me and Ned, we pooled already. We don't know shit."

"Got anything to add to that?" the detective asked his client.

"Only that it's pretty sure Renita used a pay phone really close to town. Within just a few minutes of her parents' house. If we knew what phone, maybe it would tell us what direction they were heading."

"Okay, that's something," Amsterdam said hopefully, though he knew damn well it wasn't much.

After a moment, Ned said, "I know one more thing. Don't know if it matters. My brother, first time he got to Key West, before he bolted to Naples, he ditched the mobster's car and money at a construction site."

"*What* construction site?" asked Amsterdam.

"He didn't say. Typical for him. Or maybe he didn't even know where he was. He'd just hit town. He was pretty panicked."

Amsterdam shot a questioning look at Bert.

"Construction site," the old man said. "Shit. Could be anywhere. Construction sites all over lately. Whole island's one big construction site."

"Still, it's a start. I mean, you'd think at some point he'd go back for the cash."

"Yeah, probably," Bert agreed. "I mean, how many people leave two hundred grand sitting out someplace to rot? Plus, it's let's say well established that the guy likes cars. If he liked this car enough to steal it once, maybe he'd go back to steal it again."

"What kind of car is it?" Amsterdam asked Ned.

The twin brother shook his head apologetically. "Don't know. He didn't say."

"Not a problem," the retired Mafioso said. "Look, consider the whaddyacallit, socio-economic status and typical tastes of the rightful owner. It's gonna be one of a handful of prestige brands. Dark color. Late model. New York plates." He started to rise, giving himself a head start in the slow and arduous process of emerging from his chair. "Come on, let's go find the fucking thing."

Amsterdam, unhappily remembering that this was his case too and he was pledged to help, said, "Okay, Ralph and me, we'll go look for pay phones."

32.

Back on the trawler, Renita sat in a lengthening pool of shade thrown by the pilot house. Her back was lightly pressed against the structure and her long legs were extended straight in front of her. Out of the blue, she said, "It's a shame we can't make love."

Richie was caught off guard by the sudden statement and it took a couple heartbeats for excitement to catch up with sheer surprise. Then he said, "Who says we can't?"

"Me. I say we can't. Which is a shame. It'd probably be nice. But not here. Not like this. Not on the run, hiding out, feeling like any second something bad could happen. That's not the way it should be."

He didn't argue the point.

With her ankles close together, she let her feet sweep side to side, like a metronome. Then she said, "You done it much? Made love, I mean?"

"Made love? Not exactly the way I'd put it. Not so far, at least. Had some fun sex here and there."

"Ever been in love?"

He pursed his lips and stared out at the water. Close to shore it looked black and had spikes of grass poking up through it; farther out it was pale green with floury white sand stirred in. "Not that I know of," he said. "Maybe I was and didn't realize. Maybe it's not something I'd notice. Or not till it had been and gone, then maybe I'd notice I missed it. You?"

"Yeah, I was in love once. Didn't last long."

Richie didn't ask for more details. Guys generally didn't.

"Name was Justin," Renita went on anyway. "Real old-school gentleman. Little things. Opened the car door for me. Offered me his arm. Went out of his way to show me a nice time. Very considerate. Very sweet."

Not quite managing to keep a hint of bitterness out of his voice, Richie said, "And I'll bet he was rich, too."

"Yeah, he was. Very. Fabulous car. Family mansion on the beach. But you know what? That wasn't the important part. I see that now. He opened the car door for me. Who cares what kind of car it was? We walked out on the pier. You don't have to be rich to walk out on a pier. We were going to ride bicycles together. Anyone can ride a bicycle. He didn't have to be rich."

"Guess he thought he did," said Richie. "Guess he overplayed it. Sorry it didn't work out."

"Yeah…Well…Guess it was too good to be true. Probably I should've realized that from the start instead of getting all swept up. I did get all swept up, you know. Like, crazy all swept up."

"I noticed. It was a little much, if you must know. Totally threw me off my game."

"Which I'm taking as a compliment."

"Yeah, you should."

They sat quietly for some moments. Fish moved in the

shallows; water stretched to trace out the shapes of their backs. Faint engine sounds—outboards from boats in the channel, diesels from trucks on the highway—leaked in from the distance; they were familiar noises, everyday noises, but to the fugitives in their isolation they sounded suddenly foreign, indecipherable signals from a different world. At some point, with the taken for granted litheness of the young, Renita pulled her legs in snug against her torso, circled her shins with her forearms, and laid her cheek against her knees. "So what do you think you'll do from here? When this hiding out part is over, I mean."

"Don't know. Whatever I'm doing, I'll probably be doing it in jail. Folding laundry. Counting plastic knives in the kitchen. Trying to come up with a next scheme or two."

"So you really are a pro at this? Professional liar? Full-time con-man?"

"Yup."

She brushed some hair back from her forehead. "No offense, Richie, but that's kind of a waste."

Softly but sardonically, he said, "Waste of what?"

"Oh, I don't know. Your talent. Your ambition."

He was already shaking his head. "Listen, Renita, no false modesty, okay? I happen to know I have some talent. Kind of a lot of talent, actually. But you know what my talent is for? *Seeming.* Not being. Not doing. Seeming. And the problem with seeming is that it just can't last for long. Doesn't hold up to scrutiny, to circumstance. Because there's really nothing there. It's like a reflection on water. Close enough to the real thing until the wind blows or someone throws a rock in, and then it just dissolves. Like it never existed. 'Cause it never did."

Renita badly wanted to disagree, wanted for the sake of her own memories to plead the case that the charming, gracious

Justin had been real, but she couldn't find the words to do it, especially in that place where truth-telling was the only rule. Maybe Richie in his secret heart was also hoping she would contradict him, find a way to persuade them both that there'd been at least a kernel of the actual in the fake prince he'd been portraying. But she said nothing, the moment slipped away, and the con man, swallowing his disappointment, went on blithely.

"And you? What'll you do when we bust out of here?"

She managed a brief laugh. "Who knows? I might be in jail, too."

"You won't be."

"Accessory after the fact, remember?"

"No one'll blame you for what happened, Renita. I was bluffing when I said that. Trying to scare you. Trying to control you. Sorry."

She held his eyes an extra heartbeat, then she shrugged. "That's okay. I kind of knew you were. I played along. It was kind of exciting, I admit it...So anyway, if it isn't jail I guess it's Tallahassee. Back to school. Lectures. Papers. If I'm lucky, maybe I'll get a date now and then."

"Online suitors?" Richie asked.

"Nah, I think I might be done with that. Might stick with guys I've actually met. Guys I've seen once or twice in person before getting all revved up. Guess that probably means schoolboys. 'S'gonna seem pretty tame."

"Nothing wrong with tame. Beats the hell out of phony."

"Yeah, I guess," she said without much enthusiasm or hope. But then she looked off at the shining water, and something about the gleam and twinkle of it brought the dreaminess back into her voice. "Sure would be nice, though, if there was someone not too tame, but solid, real, honest, and with a face I like as much as I like yours."

33.

"Christ, there's a lotta cranes and bulldozers and dust around," said Bert the Shirt. "Gets harder and harder to remember this town's an island."

They were inching through traffic up on the Boulevard. Ned was at the wheel now, as driving had become a nerve-wracking experience not only for Bert but for all other drivers in his vicinity. So he deferred to the young man with the fresh eyes and quicker reflexes, while he himself sat low in the deep bucket of the passenger seat, holding his dog more tightly than he really had to, afraid that on some unimaginable impulse the chihuahua would fling itself out the window and be flattened by an RV or a rented Mustang.

"Used to be," he went on, "ya saw the water from almost everywhere. Ya saw the ocean, ya saw the Gulf. Ya saw inlets, salt ponds, buoys, masts. Y'always remembered you were on an island. Now? S'gettin' to look like fuckin' Manhattan. Who in Manhattan ever notices for fifteen seconds that they happen to be surrounded by water?"

Ned didn't answer. He'd only been half-listening. As he drove he was scanning both sides of the roadway for construction sites. There were in fact a lot of them, maybe a dozen in the handful of miles they'd driven, and they all looked more or less alike: Holes in the ground with soupy gray muck at the bottom; cement mixers trembling and churning, their fat striped bodies spinning endless spirals; steam-shovels grabbing epic spoonfuls of earth and dropping them somewhere else. It was awfully tough to figure why a panicked fugitive would choose one site over another to stash a stolen car and a satchel of money.

Ned said as much to Bert. The old man didn't entirely agree.

"Difficult, yeah," he said. "But unless his decision was purely and totally random, which honestly I doubt in the case of your brother, who seems a stickler for many small details even when he's screwing up royally, there must be some kind of logic in the works here. We just gotta gather or let's say psych out or infer what this particular logic might be."

"Right. Sure. Great," said the distracted Ned, as he tried simultaneously to thread his way through Bert's syntax and Florida's appalling road mix of geriatrics, yahoos, and tourists with no idea where they were. Scooters veered suicidally from lane to lane. Horns blared just for the hell of it. They were practically out of town by now.

"So let's set the scene, or if you prefer a fancier word meaning the same thing with an Italian accent, the scenario. Your brother gets to Key West. Phone rings in the glove box. What does he do?"

"We been through this, Bert. He ditches the car and bolts to Naples."

"Right. But what we ain't been through is how he gets there. Plane? Not likely. No direct flights. Photo ID possibly a problem. Ferry? One boat a day, afternoon, it's evening by the time he gets here. So...easiest way? Safest way? Probably by bus. There's a Greyhound station over by the airport."

By then they were on Stock Island, leaving the airport and bus station ever farther behind. Fighting back exasperation and the stomach-burn of road rage, Ned said, "But he said he left the car at a construction site. You're saying you think he left it at the Greyhound station?"

At that point Bert addressed his comments to the dog, whose toenails were clicking lightly against the window frame. "What am I gonna do with this guy, Nacho? It's like pullin' teeth getting him to think like a felon." To Ned, he said patiently, "Nah, not *at* the Greyhound station. Use your noodle. He's drivin' a nice new fancy car. He parks it and gets on board a bus? Woulda looked strange. Woulda drawn attention."

"So you think—"

"I don't think nothin'. I gave up thinking long ago. But try this on for size. He's heading into Key West on the A1A. He woulda driven right past the bus station. So he'd know where it was. Then comes the ding-a-ling-a-ling, and he freaks. With me so far?"

Ned nodded and kept driving north.

"Meanwhile he's practically surrounded by all the building sites around the airport. New condos, more hotels. It's dark, they're deserted. So he picks one *near* the Greyhound station, hides the money, leaves the car. Now he's walking distance to the bus. But not just any walking distance. Walking distance through dust and muck so he gets there looking like one more local vagabond or dirtbag moving up the line. Inconspicuous. Off to Naples. Whaddya think?"

Ned said, "What I think is we've been driving in the wrong direction for half an hour. You couldn't have come up with this a little sooner?"

"Can't rush logic," Bert said placidly. "Logic takes its time. What say we turn around and check out by the Greyhound station?"

"Used to be one up at Stick and Stein," Ralphie mused from behind the wheel of his County pickup truck as he and Pete continued their futile circuit through Key West looking for a pay phone. "Booth got busted in a fight. Butt of a pool cue went right through. I don't think they ever cleaned the glass up off the seat."

Amsterdam murmured a vague acknowledgment but his attention was elsewhere. He was peering discreetly but intently at the side-view mirror.

"Then there was one on a post in Bayview Park," the mosquito man went on. "There was a mysterious guy who hogged it, always said he was talking to his agent in L.A. Some drunk trashed that one, trying to get the change out. Left it dangling by a couple of wires. Those are the only two I can think of. Know of any more?"

"Hm?" said Amsterdam. "No, I don't know of any more." He rubbed his forehead just below the hairline, then added casually but not without a hint of grimness, "But I do know we're being followed."

Ralphie's eyes darted from the rear-view mirror to his side-view with its wide-angle insert. "Shit."

Two cars back on Truman Avenue was a dark Lincoln whose tinted windows were the sinister violet of clouds that held tornadoes. The mere sight of the vehicle, low and wide behind them, was enough to give Ralphie a flashback of fear and rage that made his skin prickle. "Those bastards," he went on. "They said it was up to me to call them. Said they'd wait to hear."

"Guess they're the impatient type," said Amsterdam. "Or just not very trusting."

Ralphie maneuvered slowly through the traffic. The Lincoln held its distance like a stalking wolf. "So what do we do now?"

This was said imploringly, but also with a certain naïve

confidence that Amsterdam, being a detective and all, must deal all the time with being tailed by cars stuffed with murderous thugs. In fact the situation was as novel to him as to his client. "Um," he said haltingly, "I think maybe we should wave."

"Wave?"

"Wave. A big nice friendly wave. Just so they know we know they're there."

"I dunno," said Ralphie. "Might piss them off."

Trying to sound braver than he felt, Amsterdam said, "Hey, if it does, it does. Besides, how much more pissed off can they get?" Warming to his own idea, he lowered his window and, with unaccustomed *brio,* wagged his bare arm out in the sunshine.

Renita's uncle pressed his lips together, hesitated, and then he waved too. A mere wave of the hand may not have been a grand heroic act, but he had to admit it felt kind of good to be going on offense in some small way, baiting the bullies, defying them. A wave was a slightly more civil way of giving them the finger, and it provided the first small inkling that the best, the only, the inevitable way to defeat the murderers was not to dodge them but to fight back.

Two cars behind, the Lincoln answered the wave with a tiny lurch and for just an instant its engine sound changed from a purr to a growl.

34.

"What time you think it is?" Renita asked. She was squinting toward the west, across the flat green water of Garrison Bight to the hazily shimmering marina on the other side. The sun had changed from searing white to butter yellow and was grazing the tops of the taller masts.

Richie just shrugged.

"Kind of weird, not knowing," she went on. "I mean, no phones, no clocks, no nothing."

He shrugged again.

"Eight o'clock will be our one day anniversary," she said. "Eight on the dot." Then she gave a short, soft laugh. "Some anniversary, right? Twenty-four hours together. One quick kiss. Bunch of lying. Lotta sirens. I guess we won't even know when eight o'clock is."

Richie said nothing.

Renita said, "I wonder if you'll still be here at eight o'clock."

He shaded his eyes to gauge the angle of the sun. Very matter-of-factly, he said, "If it's dark enough by then, probably I won't be."

"Gee, you don't have to get all gooey and sentimental about

it."

He let that pass.

"So where will you head?"

"No idea. And if I knew, I wouldn't tell you. Nothing good could come of it. Besides, I won't really be anywhere. I'll just be running. That's what I do. I have some fun, I make a mess, I run away."

She considered that a moment. A breeze raised a quiet parade of ripples that marched in perfect step across the water. Weighing her words, trying not to challenge, she said cautiously, "Maybe you could stop."

His face tightened when she said that, his handsome square chin jutting out. Looking away, he said, "No. I can't."

The simple words were bitten off hard, as though to pinch off further discussion. But after a moment he himself went on more softly. "I've thought about it, Renita. You don't think I've thought about it? I can't do it. Or maybe I should say I just don't want to. Having just one name? Being the same guy every day? The thought of it creeps me out, to tell the truth. I think I'd be bored to death."

"Bored sometimes, sure," she conceded. "Everybody is. It's not the worst thing in the world. But the life you have now—"

"*Lives,*" he interrupted.

Her breath caught at that. "Ah, so that's it? You think you can have more than one?"

"I think I can try."

"But you can't," she insisted, caution falling away, replaced moment to moment by a bracing sense of how much could be allowed in their little bit of remaining time together. "Come on,

Richie, don't kid yourself. You only get one life. Just like everybody else. You can change names, change accents, it's still the same life."

"Not to me, it isn't. To me it's different every caper."

"Is it?" she ventured on. "Is it really? I don't think so. Look, you've said it yourself. It's the same deal over and over. Always running, always letting people down, never letting yourself care too much. It's just different versions of the same song."

She broke off, feeling like probably she'd said too much, expecting argument, denials, anger. But the con man didn't seem to take offense; in fact he looked oddly relieved. His taut shoulders eased and there was something in the widening of his eyes and softening of his jaw that might even have suggested gratitude, the gratitude a person feels for being unflinchingly looked at, and understood. Without rancor, he said, "Well, maybe it's the only song I know. Or maybe I'm just not tired of it yet."

35.

At the construction sites up near the airport, it was getting to be quitting time. Hammering stopped, compressors were shut down; moment by moment the din of building was subsiding as tools were put away in metal lockboxes behind the cabs of pickups.

Ned and Bert loitered at the sites' perimeters, looking more or less like unsuccessful pimps in the ancient Eldorado, slowly cruising back and forth on A1A as the workers filed out. The workers drove old Chevys, Jeeps without doors, small trucks with monster tires; some burned rubber and spit gravel as they pivoted onto the asphalt.

When the homeward tide had ebbed, Ned eased the Caddy down one unpaved path after another, venturing in for closer looks. Some of the in-progress buildings were naked frames with late vermilion sunshine now slicing in between the two-by-fours; some had concrete pillars with tendrils of re-bar sticking out the top like birthday candles. There were security patrol vehicles here and there. There was nothing that looked like it might be the stolen car of a violent New York mobster.

Then there was.

It was a dark green Jaguar, not brand new but close enough, not exactly hidden, since in the scrubby flatness there really wasn't anyplace to hide it, but pulled far enough off the access road that it wouldn't be in anybody's way and would probably be taken for one of those unexplained curiosities—never ask, never tell—that sometimes showed up at construction sites. The car was pretty well covered with coral dust and birdshit; other than that it appeared undamaged. The license plate said Empire State.

Ned climbed out of the Caddy and tried the door. It was locked. He peered through the windshield. There were some food wrappers and coffee cups tossed here and there; the glove box still gaped open, though there was nothing to be glimpsed inside, and besides, Ned had no idea what he was supposed to be looking for.

He shifted his attention to the cluster of half-built buildings maybe eighty yards away. Some of the buildings had cement floors that still looked wet; the angles of their walls and roofs were as complex as a hive. Frustrated and bewildered, he finally said, "Hell, Bert, I have no idea what to do about the car and I have no idea how to figure out where the money is."

"Fuck the money," the old man said placidly, still nestled in the passenger seat and cradling his dog. "Finding the money, that's not your job. That's your brother's job."

"Yeah, but my brother isn't here. That's the whole problem, remember?"

"Don't be a wiseguy. Course I remember. Point is, if we ever manage to get your brother out here, he'll have a car key and he'll know how to find the cash. Unless it's buried in a foundation by now. Or sealed up in a wall. Which would be unfortunate and a waste, but stuff happens."

"Okay," said Ned, working hard to track the old man's serpentine thought process. "Okay. So let's say we somehow get him out here. He digs up the money, we clean up the car, we give it all back to Marco, and we're done?"

Bert looked at him as though he'd just stepped out of a flying saucer and had not a shred of knowledge about the ways of earthlings. "Done? Of course we're not done. Not even close. Case like this, you can't just make whaddyacallit, retribution."

"Restitution."

"Whatever. Look, your brother embarrassed Marco. People know. It's public. It's an insult. That's a totally separate thing from giving him his shit back."

Ned dropped his eyes then squinted off toward the skeletal buildings, the ever-redder sunlight revealing the frailty of their wooden bones. "So you're saying Marco's gonna want to kill my brother anyway?"

"Of course," said Bert with a somewhat maddening calm. "Of course he is."

His voice thinning out to a half-strangled wheeze, Ned said, "Then what the fuck was the point of tracking down the car?"

"The car? The car is gonna be your brother's getaway. If he gets to get away, that is. If he doesn't get to get away, then a getaway car would be superfluous plus it wouldn't do him any good because he wouldn't be goin' nowhere. But I'm hoping maybe he gets to get away."

Rather hopelessly, Ned said, "And what's the use of that? If it's like you say, Marco and his thugs would be right behind him, still hunting him down."

"Yeah, that would be their tendency. Keep chasing. Get the job done. Unless they were prevented from so doing."

"Prevented?"

Bert paused, then lightly patted the empty driver's seat at his left. In a tone that could be called paternal, except that it was more tender and less commanding than the way that fathers usually talked to sons, he said, "Ned, come on, get back in the car. Please. We gotta talk."

The young man did as he was asked.

"Something you need t'understand," Bert went on. "Situation like this—threats, insults, vendettas—it's a very tough game. Crazy tough. Stupid tough. Tough to get it settled without someone dies. Or several someones. That's just the way it tends to play."

"But—"

Bert shushed him with the lift of a crinkled yellow hand. "Maybe it doesn't have to come to that. But trust me, I been there, chances are it does. And if it does, ya can't stop it, the best ya can hope for is to have some say about who wins and who loses. It's usually not pretty. Not easy to get over. I'm sayin' this so you have a little time to get used to the idea. Okay?"

Ned glanced sideways at the old man then sucked in a deep breath spiced with salt and seaweed and construction dust and let it out very slowly. "Okay."

"Now let's get to the beach," said Bert the Shirt. "I think we got a little while till the sun goes down."

36.

The Town Car full of murderers was idling at one end of the dusty parking lot of a convenience store on Stock Island. It was Bats' turn at the wheel and he was sick of it. His shiny pants were sticking to the seat, his balls weren't setting quite right between his beefy thighs, and he was getting very cranky. "Shit," he said, "I need some cigarettes."

Soup said, "Now? Now you need cigarettes? Unprofessional. I mean, we're tailin' these guys."

"Right. And they know we're tailin' 'em, and they been wavin' out the window at us for like an hour, and meanwhile I'm having a nicotine fit and I'd really like to get some fucking cigarettes, okay?"

From the back seat Marco growled, "Fine, fine, get your goddamn cigarettes. Better than listening to ya bitch about it."

At the other end of the parking lot, Ralphie was nibbling his poison-stained fingernails while waiting in his truck. Pete Amsterdam had gone into the store to ask if anyone remembered seeing a green Nissan driven by a young woman who might have used the outdoor pay phone early that morning. The clerk, surly but curious, asked Amsterdam if he was a cop or a narc or something. He told the kid don't worry, he wasn't.

Bats came in at that point and lumbered toward the counter with the telltale forward lean and shelf-scanning gaze of someone in the grip of a bad craving. He gave Amsterdam a quick dismissive glance along with a ghastly parody of a smile, just a spasmodic lift of his upper lip designed to show his canines. He stepped up way too close to the detective, didn't quite shoulder him aside but cut off his angle to the register.

Like a sumo wrestler, Amsterdam adjusted his balance to give himself some space without the implicit surrender of actually moving his feet. Absurdly, not moving his feet felt very important at the time, a matter of self-respect. With an acid politeness, he said to the clerk, "Why don't you help this gentleman first. He seems to be in a hurry."

Bats sidled in closer still, leading with an elbow. He said to Amsterdam, "And why don't you stop waving out the window like a fucking jackass."

Amsterdam smiled pleasantly. The big man bought his cigarettes, gave the detective a last carnivorous snarl, and headed for the door. His fingers trembled a bit as he wrestled with the cellophane on the package.

Amsterdam started over with the clerk, who clearly didn't want to help. His shift hadn't started till noon. He didn't know how to reach the morning person. That was the end of the conversation.

Out in the pickup truck, Ralphie didn't need to ask if Pete had learned anything of use. He could see in his face that he'd come up empty. He pulled onto the highway and looked off toward the west. It was maybe half an hour before sunset; the sun was already getting tangled up in trees and the encroaching eaves of houses. Ralph had made himself believe that his niece would surely be found that day. The approach of evening scared him. Trying to keep the fear out of his voice, he said, "Well, I think we're out of pay phones. What now?"

It was the sort of question Amsterdam dreaded because it

exposed his basic helplessness. Why did people imagine he was any better at solving their problems than they themselves would be? He was just about to shrug when Ralphie's old-school dispatch radio suddenly crackled into life. He picked up the handset.

"Yeah, this is Ralph."

"Ralph. Sophie. Listen, I know it's late but I just got a call from a really pissed off owner who happens to be a generous campaign contributor. Furious. Says she getting eaten alive. Can you possibly stop by?"

"Sure, sure," said the mosquito man, grateful for at least a small distraction from his worry.

"Just a quickie," promised the dispatcher. "PFU job."

"Yeah. Fine. Where?"

She gave him the address. It was on Hilton Haven Drive.

🌴 🌴 🌴

Renita had found a stub of pencil and a few sheets of very soggy paper in the navigation table of the trawler's cabin, and she was in the midst of drawing for Richie a very simple map. "We're sort of here," she said, pointing to a thin crescent of peninsula. "U.S. 1's just over here, a quarter, maybe a third of a mile away. Left on 1 and you're heading up the Keys."

"Where's the airport from here?"

At that Renita could not hold back a rueful laugh. "Why? That private jet you promised me is finally showing up?"

Richie let that slide. In an odd way, he'd almost gotten to enjoy her needling. Reminders of the lies he'd told were somehow comforting, cozy, like re-readings of familiar bedtime stories. He said, "Just trying to get my bearings. You know, the scale of things. I'm kind of turned around."

She resumed her drawing. Like a kid, she tucked her tongue into the corner of her mouth as she drew. "Airport's kind of far," she said. "Not really far, just no easy way to get there. Gotta go around the hump of the island then back down again on A1A."

He dragged the tip of his index finger across the outline she'd just sketched. "No way to go direct? On foot, I mean?"

She shook her head. "There's a big salt pond. Couple of canals. You'd have to go around."

"How long would it take? An hour? More?"

"Probably about an hour. But why would you want to go up there anyway? Just takes you farther from the highway."

"Just curious about where it is."

Deliberately, schoolteacher-like, she put the pencil down. "Right. And if you can walk straight to it. And how long it takes. You starting to lie again, Richie? I think maybe you're a little out of practice. That one's kind of lame."

He glanced up from the little map and through the trawler's open doorway at the water. The angle of the sun was low enough by now that the tops of the wavelets were orange-pink and the troughs between them were a gleaming, oily black. "All right, yeah, I plan on going up there. Soon as it gets dark enough. That car I stole up in New York? I'm going to pick it up and scoot. Hoping the heat's off it by now."

She said, "Wait a second. That car you stole in New York? That crazy story about pretending to be a Russian gangster? Conning someone out of all that money? That was true?"

"Renita, I've told you nothing but the truth the whole time we've been on this fucking boat. Some of it you believed, some of it you didn't. I get that. I understand. But I've told you more true things than I've told anybody in a long, long time."

She said, "I guess I should be flattered."

"Well, yeah," he answered slowly, thinking it over as he went along. "I guess you should be. My opinion, not everyone deserves the truth. Why waste it on people who don't want it, who really don't care one way or the other, who just hear what they want to hear? Anyway, this honesty business, for me, it's been kind of interesting, a nice change of pace. Wouldn't want to make a habit of it. But okay, it has its time and place. I grant you that."

37.

"Don't think I've ever been down this street before," said Pete Amsterdam. "Funny. Lived here fifteen years, thought I'd been on every street."

"Kind of tucked away," said Ralph. "Kind of useless, really. Mangroves all around. Garbage floating. No tide flow. No wonder this lady's got bugs. My crazy old father kept a boat here years ago. Hard aground most of the time. Just as well. He was usually too drunk to run it anyway."

He drove slowly beneath the dimming canopy of trees. Here and there fronds and vines hung low enough to scratch at the pickup's roof. Forty yards behind, without even a token effort at stealth, the Town Car prowled through patches of brightness and patches of shade.

The mosquito man had already passed the narrow, angled slot in the foliage when it registered just at the fuzzy edge of his consciousness that he'd glimpsed something that did not belong back there among the palms and sedges. Begging his brain to reconstruct the image, to fill in details he'd sensed but not exactly seen, he began in the next instant to believe that what he'd half-noticed was a dull green vehicle squeezed into the underbrush. His breath caught and his first impulse was to hit the brake. He said, "Jesus Christ! I think I just saw Renita's car."

Softly but firmly, one eye on the sideview mirror, Amsterdam said, "Just keep driving, Ralphie."

187

Suddenly winded with excitement, flushing scarlet at the throat, the other man said, "I can't be sure. I just got a tiny look, a flash. But it makes sense she'd be there. At the boat. Sure it does."

"Just keep driving. Slowly. Evenly. Like nothing happened, nothing changed."

The Lincoln trailed at a steady distance. To Amsterdam it did not appear that the killers inside it had noticed the brief hitch in the pickup's pace.

To Ralph it was excruciating to feel that he was so close to his niece and had yet to do anything to help her. A vein rose up in his neck. He squeezed the steering wheel so that his knuckles bulged. He said, "I could lead them to him, Pete. I could lead them to him and this would all be over."

"Except it wouldn't be. Come on, Ralph, you know that."

"They get their guy—"

"And then they get the rest of us," the detective said. "You. Me. Renita. They'd have to. How else could it play?"

Ralphie bit his lower lip so that it went dead white all around his teeth. "So what the fuck am I supposed to do?"

Trying to sound way more confident and in control than in fact he felt, Amsterdam said, "What you're supposed to do is drive to this lady's house. Spray her bugs, have her sign your clipboard. Then we drive right back past where you think you saw the car. We don't stop, we don't slow, we don't look."

Miserably, pleadingly, Renita's uncle said, "But how can I--?"

"Ralph, listen to me. We're in pretty okay shape here. We know where your niece is. At least we think we do. The shooters don't. We're way ahead. But we're only gonna get one chance to get this right. Let's not get jumpy and blow it, okay? No mistakes. No hurry. Let's think it through and be sure we have a plan."

38.

"Excuse me," Bert the Shirt began, when they all had reconvened around the little pool in Pete Amsterdam's backyard, "but your so-called plan isn't fully baked."

It was early dusk, prime time for the mosquitoes to come out, but on this evening there were no mosquitoes left alive in the immediate vicinity. On the wooden deck and the blue tiles that ringed the pool, the dead frogs and birds and mice that Amsterdam hadn't got around to cleaning up were just beginning to decompose; their stench had not yet gotten very strong and there was something almost pleasant, sort of briny-sweet about it.

"It might be unfair and possibly a little harsh to say it's really a half-assed plan," the old man went on, "but the point is that it wouldn't solve the problem and in fact would make the problem worse."

That was the last thing Uncle Ralphie wanted to hear. It was torture for him to be sitting around jabbering while Renita remained a prisoner. His butt refused to settle back into his chair; his legs were tensed and twitchy, yearning to carry him into action, any action. Leaning far forward, he said, "What's wrong with the plan?" He pointed vaguely out toward the street where the Town Car had followed his pickup truck and now sat stubbornly parked. "The killers are still tailing me. So I lead them on a wild goose chase up the Keys. Pete and Ned go to the boat.

Pete makes sure Renita's safe, brings her to her parents. Ned picks up his brother, who blows town in the stolen Jag. What's the problem?"

The old man stroked the drowsy chihuahua laid out in his lap. "The problem," he said, "is psychology. The problem is you don't understand who you're dealing with. Look, the perversionary tactic—"

"Diversionary," Amsterdam corrected.

"Whatever. The wild goose chase part. That's the easy part. It doesn't take an Einstein to bamboozle these guys. But what then?"

The question hung in the cooling air amid the gradually ripening smell of the small dead creatures. Then Bert answered it himself.

"Look, why are we in this situation in the first place? I'll tell you why. We're in this situation because these guys are very sore losers. They got conned. They're behind in the game. They're pissed off. How do they catch up? How do they win? By doing something worse than was done to them--i.e., whacking the guy. That's how they win. Except what if the guy escapes? Now they've lost twice, they're double pissed off. But not just at the guy any more. Now they're pissed at anybody who helped the guy get away. Like his brother. Like his girlfriend's uncle who led them on a wild goose chase. Like his girlfriend's uncle's detective buddy. Like the girlfriend's parents, who by the way they know where they live. It doesn't end, ya see. It just sort of ripples out. Which is why your current plan kind of stinks."

The other men looked down at the ground. They were frustrated, wrung out, thwarted, in the throes of the heartache that comes from believing you've got a thorny problem figured out, then realizing you've got to start all over. Trying to keep the gloomy tone of defeat out of his voice, Amsterdam said, "Okay,

Bert, I see your point. But hell, you got a better idea?"

The old man rearranged the limp dog in his lap. "I thought you'd never ask."

☙ ☙ ☙

"Holy shit," said Uncle Ralph when Bert had laid it out. His palms were suddenly sweaty. The skin at the back of his neck itched like it was sprinkled with wet sand. "You really think that's what we gotta do?"

"Unfortunately, I know it is. But only if we're all in. Only if we all agree."

He glanced from under his thick gray eyebrows at the members of the small alliance. Ned Preston's diamond-shaped face had blanched, and underneath the sudden pallor was an expression of bitter irony, as if he'd always known that someday his brother's misdeeds would lead to something as desperate as this. He said, "Fuck it, I'm in."

Reluctantly, the way he said and did most things, as though all he really wanted was to sit still and quietly in a room, if only the room he was sitting in didn't keep catching on fire, Pete Amsterdam said, "Okay, me too."

Bert nodded then said to Ralphie, "Didn't you once say you had a number for these guys?"

Renita's uncle dug in his pockets for the rumpled candy wrapper Bats had given him. While he was searching, Bert said to the group, "I'm gonna take one shot at makin' nice. Just for the sake of our conscience. Just so we can say we tried."

Ralphie found the number. Squinting hard at the tiny keypad of his seldom-used phone, Bert punched it in. The others leaned forward in their chairs and got by with shallow, silent breaths.

In Bert's ear, a gruff voice said, "Yeah?"

"Lemme speak to Marco."

"And who the fuck are you?"

"Bert d'Ambrosia. From Astoria."

The others were impressed with Bert's calm and suave delivery. The effect of it was somewhat tarnished when, after a pause, the gruff voice came back on the line and said, "He says he don't know you from Adam."

This embarrassed Bert only slightly. He knew there was a whole generation out there who'd never heard of him. This was the way of the world; he didn't take it personally. "Tell him I done a fair bit of business with his Uncle Funzie. Tell him his good friends are my friends too."

That must have worked, because the next voice on the line was Marco's rather reedy, peeping tenor. "Holy crap. You're *that* Bert d'Ambrosia and you're still alive?"

"As of now, yeah. Dead men don't make phone calls. And I'm calling about this little misunderstanding that's brought you to Key West."

"Fuck's it got to do with you?"

"That's not important. But inna meantime, the guy you're looking for? So happens I might know where he is."

"Where?"

"Not so fast, okay? I'm hoping maybe we can patch this up."

"No way."

"You'll get all your losses back, Marco. Every dollar."

"Are you soft in the head, old man? Have you forgotten all the rules?"

"Whose rules, Marco?"

"Just tell me where he is."

"And what about the young lady involved?" Bert pressed. "Her uncle's a friend of mine. You promised him she wouldn't be hurt."

"Promised? I never promised him nothing."

"Then promise me."

This called forth a quick bray of a laugh from Albertini. "Promise you? Listen, gramps, neither you or your friend or the man in the moon can get me to promise them anything. It's gonna go like it's gonna go."

Bert glanced from face to face around the little gathering at the pool. Then he said into the phone, "You ever heard of forgiveness, Marco?"

"Fuck forgiveness."

"And you really think a little thing like this is worth people dying over?"

"People deserve to die, they die. It's not that big a deal, old man."

Bert paused, not for long, and said, "Okay, Marco, if you can live with it, I guess I can, too. Where you staying?"

"Flagler House. Over by—"

"I know where it is. Meet me in front of it in twenty minutes. I don't like it, but okay, outta respect for our mutual friends and because I now have a deeper understanding of the situation, I'll lead ya to the slaughter." He clicked out of the call.

For a moment no one spoke. Out on the street, a car engine

started, its sound diminishing as the vehicle pulled away. The stink of the gently rotting creatures on the pool apron had ratcheted up a notch, taken on a metallic tinge, like stale anchovies. Bert started rising from his chair. It was a labored, multi-step process involving the shifting of his dog, pressing down for leverage with his hands, slowly getting his knees to unbend, and then, last, triggering the stringy muscles that straightened his back. Finally, he said, "So I guess that's that. You guys got half an hour to do your part."

"You just told Marco twenty minutes," said Amsterdam.

"Yeah, but he don't know how slow I drive."

39.

Although Richie and Renita didn't know it, it was exactly eight o'clock, twenty-four hours from the start of this weird date that had been so full of promise, as they stood on the trawler's leaning deck to say their last goodbyes. The goodbyes weren't much. How could they be? In a one-day relationship, there just wasn't a lot to reminisce about; not even very much to regret. With a dizzyingly radical compression, they'd gone from infatuation to doubt to disillusion to blame to understanding, and even beyond that to some version of amnesty and friendship, all in one spin of the earth. Lots of couples took thirty years to do that. Lots of couples never managed it at all.

So they stood there in the satin twilight. Water lapped softly at the hull. Birds skidded on splayed webbed feet and landed at the shoreline. Richie offered an almost bashful handshake. Renita pulled him into a brief chaste hug, more comradely than passionate. "Be careful," she said, when her lips were close to his ear.

"Doubt it," he said. "And you? You'll go to your folks?"

"Guess so. For a day or two. Get some rest, go back up to school. Life goes on."

Somewhat distractedly, part of him already on the run, he nodded. He pivoted to walk away but his feet declined to move. In even the most blunt of partings there is an undecided moment, a tug toward staying just a little longer, an ache of feeling there's more that should be said. Looking at nothing, Richie said, "I'll think about you. I'll think about you for a good long time."

Then he stepped down from the trawler onto the broken dock and took one last glance back. From his low angle, Renita looked not just tall but monumental, permanent, as though if she were removed there would be a blank place in the sky behind her. He began to walk away.

He'd gone three steps over the white stones toward the narrow clearing when he heard, from somewhere deep in the foliage, a voice uncannily like his own, but pinched down into a harsh and breathy whisper, calling out his one true name. "Richie!"

He stopped, off balance, in mid-stride, at the sound. Had he really heard it? It was incongruous, wildly out of place, impossible. As if questioning the trustworthiness of reality itself, he whispered back, "Ned?"

At that, the con man's twin emerged from the last fringe of the shrubbery.

From the deck, Renita looked on, utterly bewildered, as the two perfectly matched silhouettes moved closer in the dimness. Their profiles were two halves of the same profile, as if they'd been cut out from a single folded piece of paper; their postures echoed one another as in some beguiling but disturbing mirror trick.

They met at the end of the winding row of coral slabs, and the first thing Richie said was, "What the fuck you doing here?" It was an accusation, not a welcome.

"Some people," his brother pointed out, "when an unexpected guest arrives, they say hello. Or nice to see you. Something sort of mild and polite like that."

"Come on, Ned. Cut the shit. Why the fuck you here?"

"Okay, since you want to get right down to it, I'm here to save your sorry ass."

The con man managed a low, dismissive laugh. "Save my ass? From what? From who? Look, Ned, I don't need—"

"Yeah, you *do* need," his brother interrupted, and then, without forethought, without the slightest inkling he was about it to do it, he grabbed his twin by the shoulders and shook him hard enough to make his head snap back. Now that he'd had the relief of seeing him alive, now that they were face to identical face, all he'd been through on his twin's behalf flooded back over him and made him furious. "I been worried sick about you. I been beat up, threatened, kicked around."

"Why? For what? Calm down, man! All I did, I stole a couple cars. The cops are after me. What else is new?"

"You dumb selfish bastard. You should wish it's just the cops that are after you. You have any idea who you conned up in New York?"

"Yeah. I conned some pathetic little schmuck in a strip club."

"You conned the Mob, you asshole. You conned Marco Albertini. And you're so caught up in your make-believe bullshit world, your I-can-fool-anybody world, you didn't even know the Mafia's been chasing you for a week. Smart guy. You didn't even know! You're really lucky you're not dead."

Richie gestured, started to speak, but he was still absorbing the enormity of his screw-up and no words came.

Ned caught his breath and started in on him again. With a hand that was trembling with indignation, he pointed up toward the bow of the old trawler, where Renita was still standing, rapt and baffled, leaning against a rail. "And you're lucky you didn't get her killed, too. Your hostage."

"I'm not a hostage," Renita said simply, softly. "I never was a hostage. I'm Renita."

Ned hadn't expected her to speak just then, and her quiet assurance slowed him down a bit. They looked at each other in the violet light. Everything except for the rasping of crickets stopped for the duration of the glance. Disconcertingly, irresistibly, she held his eyes a fraction longer than was usual. When he spoke again the edge in his voice was buffered. "Okay, sorry. Hostage, not a hostage, he could've got you killed. He still might get you killed. Me too. All of us."

She pondered that for a couple of heartbeats but her serene, abstracted face didn't seem to register much fear. The extreme oddness of the situation just didn't leave much room for fear, and she seemed far less focused on the possibility of being murdered than on the abrupt, miraculous, and chivalrous appearance of this new and unknown brother. Her gaze still lingering on Ned, she said to Richie, "You never told me you had a twin."

Sourly, he said, "Not something that comes up in daily conversation, okay?"

She looked at the paired heads of coarse black hair, the two sets of wide, high cheekbones, the quartet of deep-set serious eyes. "Amazing how alike you are."

"On the outside," said the con man, not bothering to hide the resentment that the bad kid always harbors toward the good kid, the envy masked by mockery that the troublemaker reserves for the model student. "Totally different on the inside. Ned's reliable. Ned's honest. Ned's a boy scout."

The con man's brother didn't rile at the taunts. He'd heard them all before. He said, "Listen, Richie, we don't have a lot of time. I'm getting you out of here."

The offer of help was galling. "I don't need you to rescue me.

I have a plan."

"Yeah, I'm sure you do. It probably involves a green Jaguar."

"You found the car?"

"Wasn't rocket science. And, unlike you, I know who owns it. There's a lot more going on than you have any idea about, Richie. A lot more people who had to get involved."

The con man chewed his lip and looked down at the pale stones beneath his feet. A faint and choked-back hint of remorse came close to breaking through. "Ned, hey, I never wanted—"

"Never wanted *what*? Never wanted anybody else to have to come clean up your messes? Maybe you should've thought of that before."

Richie said nothing. Ned dangled a car key in front of him.

"Take this. Swap it for the Jag, grab your money, and get out of town."

"But—"

"No buts, Richie. There isn't time."

The con man took the key but for a moment he didn't move.

Renita looked at the two brothers standing there a step apart, a perfectly symmetrical sliver of grainy night between them. Mother-like, she said, "Come on, guys, shake hands at least. You'll regret it if you don't."

Grudgingly at first, then with an instant of sorrowful but fierce conviction, they hugged. When they separated it was like an ink blot doubling. Richie dipped a shoulder and moved quickly toward the clearing and the rest of his bizarre and crooked life.

Ned turned his eyes up toward Renita, monumental as a

figurehead, still perched against the rail. He said, "There's some things that need explaining. You mind if we talk a little while?"

She liked his face. She felt like she already knew him. She said she didn't mind.

40.

Bert drove at a stately geriatric tempo through the streets of Key West, whose pavements were still pliant with the heat of day; the Caddy's wide tires, rolling so slowly, seemed to pull at the softened asphalt as though it were taffy. The streetlights had come on; they had throbbing orange haloes around them, and the pulsing glare only made it harder for the old man to fix the outlines of the chaotically moving objects— bicycles, cats, pedestrians—that darted back and forth in front of him. Fact was, it had been many years since he'd sat behind the wheel at night, but now it needed doing and he was not a man to shirk. So he eased along, yearning for the next red light, the next stop sign, that might give him an excuse to pause a moment, rub his eyes, regroup.

With much greater haste, Amsterdam and Ralphie were riding in the detective's square little car toward the Mosquito Control equipment yard up near the dump.

The yard was ringed by chain-link fence festooned on top with somehow Christmassy curls of razor wire. There were floodlights around the perimeter but no night watchman. The shed that held the dispatcher's office still issued forth the sickly blue glow of a computer monitor, though the dispatcher had gone home hours before.

Ralphie punched in a gate code, and a slice of spindly fence rolled away on scuffed and dusty wheels. Amsterdam pulled through the opening and toward a rank of stubby trucks whose tanks full of poison were shaped like *mortadellas*.

At the same moment, at a stark and skeletal construction site near the airport, Richie Pestucci parked his brother's crummy rented car near the end of a gravel access road, then, without hurry or stealth, he walked over to a particular half-built structure and counted in three strides from its southeast corner. He tapped on the sheetrock wall with his knuckles to find the weakest point between the studs, then, with one karate-style side-kick he bashed it in.

Pulling away some sundered pieces of pressed gypsum, he reached down into the narrow space between the slab foundation and the temporary plywood floor and removed the briefcase that held Marco Albertini's money and the key to the Jaguar. With a depth of insouciant calm reserved for saints and lifelong outlaws, he toted the loot over to the stolen car, opened the door, and tossed it in.

He was already in the driver's seat and reaching for the ignition when he decided to amend his plan.

Fumbling around in the Jaguar's glove box, he found a ball-point pen stolen from a motel chain and a Chinese menu from somewhere in Queens, and dashed off a brief note. Then he opened the briefcase, grabbed a sheaf of hundreds and stuffed the bills into his pocket, leaving the menu in their place. Without hesitation, he yanked the briefcase out of the Jag and put it in his brother's crummy renter. Finally, settled once again into the handsome stolen vehicle, he wheeled out of the access road and headed...where? He had no idea, nor did he know who he'd be when he got there.

On the deck of the old trawler, Renita and Ned were sitting in the deepening dark. Ned was shaking his head and saying, "My brother. I'm so sorry you got mixed up with him."

She shrugged. The shrug made her collarbones bow out in a way that Ned found very beautiful. "I'm not. It's been an adventure. I mean, what else would I have been doing? Studying? Going to class? Fantasizing about meeting someone different and exciting? All in all, it's been a blast."

"Amazing attitude," Ned said.

Renita did that pretty shrug again. "Only one I've got. But what you were saying to Richie, about the Mafia and all—it's true?"

"Oh yeah."

"They really want to kill him?"

"Him and anybody with him. Or anyone who helps him. Or anyone they happen to get mad at."

Renita looked up at the sky and pondered that. It was a spring sky, stars lightly misted with shimmering vapor, Gemini near the zenith, the Dipper spilling toward the west. The breeze was still. Everything was quiet.

Ned went on softly, mildly, "So it looks like we're going to have to kill them first."

"Excuse me?"

"Bert says there just isn't any other way."

"Who the hell is Bert?"

"This old Mob guy with a chihuahua. Retired. He sort of adopted me. Been advising us."

Renita weighed that, not for long, and decided that, once again, her credulity was being pushed too far and in very dubious directions. She sighed in disappointment. Ned had seemed so different, for about two minutes. Finally she said, "Does this run in your family, this making up crazy stories? Some genetic thing? I mean, you had me going for a while, but really, having to kill people? Mobsters with chihuahuas? This is way more out there even than anything your brother told me."

"Except it's true. Every word. I'm the honest one, the Boy Scout, remember? Your uncle should be here any minute."

This one shred of verifiable fact nudged her back over the fine line toward believing. "My uncle?"

"Your uncle Ralphie. He'd do anything for you, Renita."

"I know he would, but how would he even--?"

"Know you're here? Guess you haven't found out you're a celebrity. Whole thing was in the morning paper. The sunk Bentley in Naples. Your ID in the car. Little detective work, little luck. By this time, everybody knows you and my brother were holed up together, the two of you, hiding out."

"Everybody? Who's everybody?"

"The good guys, the bad guys. Everybody. And now they're on their way."

She hugged her knees as she tried to sift through all that information. "On their way...here?"

He nodded.

She said, "But why? Your brother isn't even here now."

"Right," said Ned. "But I am." He gestured up toward his diamond-shaped face and thick black hair. "Close enough, wouldn't you say?"

Renita looked at him. Her mouth went dry. She said, "So wait a second. You're gonna be—"

"Bait," he said simply.

"Bait?"

"Every trap needs some."

Her tongue went to the corner of her mouth as she tried to get her mind around the implications of the dire switcheroo. "So let me make sure I have this right. You're pretending to be your brother so people can try to kill you? That's like the kindest, bravest thing I ever heard."

"It isn't kind and it isn't brave," he said. "It's necessary. Brave and kind would be if I thought I had a choice. I don't. I'm doing this because who else could?"

"Well, I think it's amazing." She looked at him from underneath arched brows and held the stare that disconcerting instant longer than most people would, or could endure without squirming. Then she said, "I'm staying with you on the boat."

The offer was so unexpected that it took Ned a moment to find the words to turn it down. "No, you're not. Thank you, but you're not. Way too risky. And there's really no need."

"Yes, there is," she insisted. "There is a need. The bad guys think there's two people hiding out. You just said that yourself. A man and a woman. What if they only see the man? What if they get suspicious? What if the whole plan falls apart?"

Ned just shook his head. "Renita, listen, no way you're staying. I don't want you to. Plus there's no way in hell that your uncle would let you."

With finality, she said, "My uncle doesn't tell me what to do. Ever. That's how we can still be friends. I'm staying."

41.

"Can't you drive a little faster?" said Marco Albertini, as Bert crawled down the quiet street that led away from the Flagler House hotel. He'd decided to ride with the old man, his accomplices following in the Town Car.

"I could," said Bert, "but I'd hate to hit a fire hydrant or a garbage can or something. Truth is, Marco, I can't see shit. Not saying you should worry. Plus I got the dog here, you see how he's leaning on my arm, jumping on my balls. Gets a little distracting. So I'm goin' for accuracy, not speed."

They drove another block that felt like half a mile. Marco started drumming impatient fingers against the El Dorado's dashboard.

"You nervous, Marco?"

"Nervous? Nah. Just wanna get this the hell over with."

"Drumming your fingers like that. To me that says nervous."

The little mobster said nothing.

"I'd be nervous if I was you," the old man offered.

"You ain't me," said Marco.

"Threats beget threats. Violence begets violence, Marco. That's the big problem with the world. Everything ricochets.

Y'ever think about karma, Marco?"

"Parma? Where the *prosciutto* comes from? Why the fuck would I think about Parma?"

They drove the rest of the way even slower and in silence.

Small branches snapped and moths and lizards scattered as Ralph bulldozed the Mosquito Control truck as far as he dared into the undergrowth beyond the narrow clearing. Foliage scraped the windshield; the stubby poison tank was barely off the roadway. Working together, swatting at mosquitoes and fending off bats, he and Pete tugged many yards of the thick orange hose from its spool, bushwhacking toward the shoreline, using the nozzle as a bludgeon against the vines. Mangrove roots grabbed at their feet; spider webs stretched and glued themselves against their faces. When they finally reached the mucky boundary between land and water, they wrestled the hose over coral stones toward the broken dock and listing trawler.

Then Ralph abruptly dropped his part of the burden. He had to see his niece alive and well. He suddenly couldn't stand to wait even a few more seconds. He ran, splashing now and then, over the imperfect path of stones.

Renita stepped down from the trawler to meet him on the dock. Their reunion, for all the worry and emotion that had led up to it, was laconic and reserved, almost bashful, without tears or theatrics or long embraces. They kissed each other on the cheek. Ralphie held her by the shoulders, at arm's length, and appraised her. His heart was pounding in a way that secretly embarrassed him, but all he said was, "You okay?"

"Fine, Uncle Ralph. Really. I'm sorry for all the—"

"Not your fault. None of it's your fault. We'll get it all cleared up. Come on, I'll bring you to the truck for now."

At that she set her feet just very slightly wider apart and almost imperceptibly firmed her posture. "No," she said, "I'm staying on the boat."

"Renita, please. I don't think you understand—"

"I do understand. I should be here with Ned. It makes sense I'd be here. It's part of the plan."

"But it's gonna get—"

"I know how it's gonna get," she interrupted. "But all this brave stuff. All this everybody stepping up. You can't just leave me out of it. I've earned it. I'm staying."

Her uncle looked down at his feet. He started to speak but the words were stifled by a frustrating certainty that he wasn't going to win the argument, that all he could accomplish would be to make frayed nerves even more so and to waste seconds that couldn't afford to be wasted. Fretful but resigned, he kissed his niece on the cheek again and turned back toward where he'd dropped the poison hose.

By then Pete Amsterdam was walking toward them. He'd heard their exchange. He'd figured correctly how it would turn out. He was carrying two gas masks.

42.

The last mauve glow of twilight had died out in the west. On Hilton Haven Drive, the streetlamps ended thirty yards in from the junction with the highway, and after that, to Bert's old eyes at least, the darkness was annihilating. Here and there, crowns of palms suggested themselves as even darker silhouettes against a charcoal sky; now and again, the slant of a roof seemed to carve a slice through the blackness. But for the most part Bert saw nothing except the bugs that capered in front of his headlights.

"You sure you know where you're going, old man?" Marco asked him.

"Course I'm sure."

He wasn't. Ralphie had told him to look for a notch in the foliage about three, four tenths of a mile in. Told him it was easy to miss. That part turned out to be an understatement. To the left and right of the pavement, the relentless wall of shrubs and scabby trees seemed to be leaning in on him then pinching from above like the arches in a church. The Lincoln's high-beams bounced off his rear-view mirror and scalded his eyes. He squinted and crawled along.

Finally he thought he'd found the place. He nosed off the road and into the jungle. The El Dorado rocked on brittle springs; thorns and knife-edged sedges clawed at the tired paint of its panels and doors.

Marco said, "This can't be right. If you're fuckin' with us--"

The unfinished threat was wasted on Bert. He kept going. The Town Car bounced along behind, sealing off the exit, locking him in. Trying to stay calm, the old man stroked his dog with the hand that wasn't wrestling with the steering wheel.

The funneling path curved left. Just past the bend, half-enmeshed in leaves and boughs, stood a crummy old green Nissan with its license plate removed. Bert pulled to within a few inches of its bumper and switched off the Caddy's engine. Pointing beyond Renita's car, he said to Marco, "You'll find your boy down there. God forgive me for doin' this."

Without a word of thanks the little mobster sprang out of the car. Soup and Bats lifted their bulky bodies through the thrown-open doors of the Lincoln. In an instant the three killers had their guns out. The guns captured faint glints of starlight that flashed and dimmed on their twitching barrels like the flickering of fireflies.

The men slipped through the clearing toward the meandering stones that bridged the muck, and when the subsiding foliage had dropped away below eye level, Marco Albertini saw, unmistakably stamped against the deep purple of the sky, the diamond-shaped head and the square firm chin of the man he was pledged to kill. The con man. The man who'd made a fool of him.

He was standing on the deck of a ratty old boat, and the tableau was just as the assassin had pictured it in his lurid imaginings of revenge: The con man talking, laughing with his tramp of a girlfriend. Maybe laughing at him, at how he'd been duped. Maybe making plans for how they'd spend his pilfered money. For a moment the mobster just watched the galling, ghostly shapes, sickly savoring his hatred. Then, his minions close behind him, he started creeping low and silent across the muck from stone to stone.

His eyes never wandered from his quarry. So he didn't notice that Bert the Shirt, feeling his way like a sleepwalker with both hands out in front of him--one clutching his dog, the other his dinged and archaic revolver--was trailing his steps by only a few paces. He couldn't know that Pete Amsterdam was crouching in wait on the far side of the pitch-dark pilot house. He dimly saw, but made nothing of, the thick orange hose that snaked along the dock and was threaded through a scupper on the leaning boat.

Like stalking lions, the killers eased to within striking distance then broke into a lumbering sprint. They were half a dozen soggy strides from the dock when Bert whispered to the dog, "Sing, Nacho, sing!"

The chihuahua filled its tiny lungs and launched into the only trick it knew, screaming out its piercing three-note howl. *Ow-ow-OWWW! Ow-ow-OWWW!*

At the signal, Ned and Renita broke off their stagy conversation, looked up, seemed to notice the intruders for the first time, and fled into the trawler's cabin.

The thugs watched with satisfaction as their victims panicked and stupidly trapped themselves, put themselves into a corner with no place left to run. It would make their execution that much easier and quicker. Or it would have, except that Renita and Ned were already strapping on their gas masks and concealing themselves snugly behind the solid oak bulkhead of the cozy forward berth.

Pistols poised, Marco and Soup and Bats clambered up onto the dock, stumbling now and then on its snaggled planks. They reached the listing trawler and sprang aboard. In a crush of avid, musky bodies they piled through the doorway and into the obliterating darkness of the cabin.

A fraction of a second later, Pete slunk around from his waiting place, slid the door tightly shut, and leaned against it, sealed it off, with every ounce of his weight and strength.

Bert fired his antique .38 at the sky.

Hearing the shot, Uncle Ralph switched on the gas, the strong stuff that killed everything, bugs and birds and rats and people, thoroughly and quickly. Marco and his murderers were dying even before they noticed that something had gone very wrong. Blindly, futilely, in an almost poignant last attempt at winning, they fired their pistols at random; impotent bullets buried themselves in wood or infernally whanged as they glanced off old brass fittings. For some moments there were powerful poundings against the door pinched shut by Amsterdam's straining shoulder, but the hammering soon weakened into pathetic sounds of clawing and scratching, louder versions of how rodents say goodbye when trapped in walls. Then the night went uncannily quiet except for the diminishing hiss of the poison as the pressure in the valve subsided.

When even that whisper had trailed away, there came a gentle tapping on the inside of the cabin door. Amsterdam relaxed and opened it. Stepping carefully over three sprawled and lifeless bodies, Ned and Renita emerged. The detective asked if they were all right. They said they were fine, their voices sounding like kazoos through the gas masks.

They didn't seem to realize at first that they were holding hands, holding hands not in the way that merely brushed palm against palm but in the more resolute and bonded way that made all their fingers intertwine. Later, neither would be able to say which one of them had reached out for the other. They only knew that somehow it had happened.

EPILOGUE

I t fell to Amsterdam to dispose of the bodies. Not a pleasant chore, but not especially difficult either. With help from Ralphie and Ned, he loaded the still-warm corpses into the trunk of the Town Car, then drove, alone, a dozen miles up the Keys to where the swift-running Shark Channel coursed beneath a little-used bridge. Three splashes later, the outgoing tide was carrying the polluted bodies to deep water where the hammerheads and barracudas weren't very picky as to diet.

By the time the dead guys had bobbed and pinwheeled away, Bert's old Caddy, driven now by Ned, had pulled up onto the bridge. Amsterdam turned the Lincoln's steering wheel slightly to the left and secured it in that position with his belt. A good nudge from the El Dorado over the hump of the bridge and toward the downward slope was enough to send the Town Car swerving through the flimsy guardrail and nose-first into the drink. Just for a moment, the vehicle balanced in a somehow clownish, trembling headstand. Then the current pushed it over onto its roof, the back tires lazily and questioningly spinning, as if wondering where the road had gone.

On the drive to the construction site down near the airport, wind whistled softly, prettily, through the stuck mechanism of the Caddy's convertible top, but the mood in the car was very somber. Ned and Pete, still in shock about what had transpired and the parts they'd played in it, sat in contemplative or maybe just exhausted silence. Bert, more experienced, more pragmatic, and far less sentimental about the untimely deaths of three really awful men, finally said, "Come on, guys, cheer up. They had it coming. They left us no choice. We gave 'em every chance."

Neither Ned nor Pete could muster a response, so Bert turned his attention to the innocent dog. "And you did your part beautiful, didn't ya, Nacho? Ya did perfect. Sang right on cue. Like Sinatra ya sang."

The dog licked the old man's fingers and danced on his crotch as Ned turned off of A1A and onto the construction access road.

The access road was made of pale, pearly gravel and it shimmered like a satin ribbon in the starlight. Ned found his crummy rented car unlocked, the ignition key casually tossed onto the floor mat. He'd started the car and put it in gear before he noticed the briefcase propped in the passenger seat. It should have occurred to him at once that the briefcase was stuffed with Marco Albertini's money; but it did not occur to him because he simply could not imagine that his brother Richie would give him anything. Richie took. Ned gave. Again and again. That was the deal. That was their life story.

So his mind was confused and his fingers strangely numb when he snapped open the latches of the briefcase. The bills were for the most part neatly stacked, with a few loose hundreds scattered and fanned out on top. But what caught Ned's eye was a hand-scrawled note written with a rushed and radical economy on the back of a Chinese take-out menu. It said: *That bail money. Yeah, I remember. Sorry. Here's some interest. School?*

🌴 🌴 🌴

It took Ralphie a few minutes to re-spool the long and twisted orange hose. Now and then the nozzle hung up on a root and the mosquito man had to hack his way into the foliage to free it. When this happened, the bugs, as though gloating over a rare chance for vengeance in an ancient grudge, attacked his hands and wrists and ears. He accepted the bites and stings as a kind of penance, and he carried himself with the stony and grave composure of a man who knows he's done something terrible but also knows he did it with a pure heart and for the best possible reasons.

They decided to leave Renita's car just where it was, since it was still being looked for by police; eventually there'd be some explaining to do, some strings to pull with the local authorities. In the meantime, the young woman rode with her uncle as he returned the poison truck to the equipment yard. She was somewhat dazed, of course, though less so than she would have been a day or two before, before this weird blind date had stretched her sense of what was possible, had made the bizarre seem almost normal and the unthinkable nearly routine. Her voice soft, a bit hollow at first, she said to her uncle, "I can't believe you did all this for me."

Never taking his hands off the wheel or his eyes off the road, he just gave a modest shrug.

"I mean, I *can* believe it," his niece went on. "I knew you'd be there for me. I'm just sorry it got so crazy."

He shrugged again and said, "It's all okay." Then he added, almost shyly, "But Renita, there's one thing I'd really like if you would do for me."

"Anything. Of course."

"When you see your parents, be nice to them. Please. They feel really guilty."

"I doubt that," Renita said, without rancor but not without hurt.

Ralphie, usually not confident about matching words to feelings, ventured on this time. "They're so mean to each other.

They blame each other, needle each other. Why would they do that unless, deep down, they blamed themselves, felt guilty that they weren't better parents, didn't give you more? Try to help them feel a little better, okay?"

At the equipment yard, he maneuvered the poison truck into formation with the others and picked up Pete Amsterdam's small, square car that had been left behind. He drove to the detective's house, getting there just as the others were arriving. Amsterdam proposed a round of drinks to calm the nerves and lighten the mood. They tried to sit outside by the swimming pool, but the stink of dead creatures around it had thickened with the night and taken on a skunky edge. Bert very tentatively poked at a stiff frog with the toe of his pointy shoe. "Shoulda cleaned 'em up before they got glued to the deck," he said to his host. "Gonna be a messy bastard now."

They retreated to the living room. Ralphie took the chair that already felt like his because he'd sat there twice before. Bert chose a wicker rocker and balanced his dog on the wide arm of it. Ned and Renita sat side by side on a sofa, their legs parallel, hips just very lightly touching. Amsterdam passed beers around.

Ralphie said, "So this makes you, what, Pete? Two for two on detective cases?"

"I guess," he said. Then he added modestly but also accurately, "And I haven't detected a single thing yet."

"Maybe next time," Bert put in. "Ya know, practice makes perfect."

Amsterdam was shaking his head. "There won't be a next time. I quit. I'm retired."

"Retired," the old man said dismissively. "What the hell's retired mean? Look, I been retired thirty-something years. It doesn't mean ya don't do nothing. It means ya relax, rest up till there's something to be done. Then ya do it. Then ya go back to resting."

It might have been the mention of that word that made Renita finally give in to a delicious and undisguisable yawn. The chihuahua yawned in sympathy. That made Bert yawn also. Not wanting to admit he was more tired than anybody, he said to Renita, "Jeez, hon, you must be beat."

She managed a soft and sleepy smile. "Yeah, I am."

In that instant Ned sensed the opportunity he hadn't quite realized he'd been waiting for. "Can I drive you home?"

🌴 🌴 🌴

Out on the street, under the pink-orange haloes of the streetlights and amid the distant whine of scooters and the rustling of palms, Ned opened the passenger side door for her. Impressed by the gesture, she said, "Oh boy, another gentleman."

"Hm?" he said distractedly. "Oh. The door. I did that because I had to move the briefcase."

"And honest, too," she said, as she slipped into the cramped and very unglamorous rented car.

Offhandedly, he said, "I had to move the briefcase 'cause it's full of money." He closed her door and walked around to the driver's side.

"Seriously?" she said when he was settled in behind the wheel.

"My brother left it for me. His way of apologizing."

"Funny guy, your brother. Complicated."

"Yup."

He started the car and headed down the street. After a

moment, she said, "But you know what? Let's not talk about him anymore. Let's talk about you. What'll you do now that this is finished? What'll you do with all that money?"

He scratched an ear. "Haven't had much time to think about it. What I probably should do is go back to school. Didn't finish the first time. Ran out of dough."

"What were you studying?"

He gave a brief and muffled laugh. "Forensic psychology. Hoping to grasp the mysteries of the criminal mind."

She hesitated for a couple of heartbeats, trying to decide if she should trust herself, trying to measure how bold she should be. Then she said, "Pretty good program for that up in Tallahassee."

He didn't answer right away, but he kept looking sideways at her. As the car passed under streetlamps, one by one, the light slid over her, revealing her from lap to chin, the strong shoulders, the graceful collarbones, then dimming out until the next lamp had been glided under. It was a thrumming, slinking sort of light and it made her look almost like she was dancing in her seat. It made him so happy to look at her that he forgot it was his turn to speak.

Finally she said, "That was sort of an invitation. I mean, it could sort of be taken that way. Did you pick up on that at all?"

"I hoped that's what it was."

"You could come visit, check it out. We could get to know each other...Although, can I tell you something weird? We met, what, an hour or two ago? I feel like I know you already."

He gestured toward his chin, "Well, the face—"

"The face, sure," she said. "But that's not what I'm talking about. I mean the inside. The real part. I felt like I knew the real part of you in about ten seconds."

"Guess that makes me the uncomplicated one."

"Nothing wrong with that."

They drove, night air swooshing softly through the car. Ned wished the ride could go on for a long time, but Key West is a tiny island and they were already coming to the quiet locals' neighborhood that included Jamaica Drive. He glided to the curb in front of Renita's parent's house. He put the car in Park, which was as much as he could think of to do to stretch the moment at least a little. Then he sat there, wanting to touch her shoulder, to put his arm around her, but with his bashful hands stuck fidgeting on the steering wheel.

She said, "Ned, there's just one more thing I have to say about your brother, then I'm really done with it. I kissed him once. Do you mind?"

He shrugged. Of course he minded.

"It didn't really count," she went on. "Wasn't much of a kiss. One-way. A peck on the cheek. I kind of snuck up on him, to tell the truth. It was something a kid would do, a naïve little girl pretending she was on a dream date. I sort of knew it wasn't real. But I wanted so badly to believe it was. I think I've grown up a little bit since then. Understand?"

He nodded. He wondered if he could reach for her without having it seem like sneaking up, without acting like a kid on a date. He reached out very slowly, cautiously, and stroked her hair.

She didn't resist the caress but she didn't melt into it either. She smiled and held his gaze for that disconcerting extra fraction. Then she opened the car door and starting leaning toward her parents' house. Looking back, she said, "Next time I kiss someone, I want it to be totally the opposite of that. Two-way. No pretending. Real. Kind of like the way it felt when we wound up holding hands. So maybe I'll see you up in Tallahassee. Okay?"

ABOUT THE AUTHOR

Laurence Shames has been a New York City taxi driver, lounge singer, furniture mover, lifeguard, dishwasher, gym teacher, and shoe salesman. Having failed to distinguish himself in any of those professions, he turned to writing full-time in 1976 and has not done an honest day's work since.

His basic laziness notwithstanding, Shames has published more than twenty books and hundreds of magazine articles and essays. Best known for his critically acclaimed series of Key West novels, he has also authored non-fiction and enjoyed considerable though largely secret success as a collaborator and ghostwriter. Shames has penned four New York Times bestsellers. These have appeared on four different lists, under four different names, none of them his own. This might be a record.

Born in Newark, New Jersey in 1951, to chain-smoking parents of modest means but flamboyant emotions, Shames graduated summa cum laude from NYU in 1972 and was inducted into Phi Beta Kappa. Shortly after finishing college, he began annoying editors by sending them short stories they hated. He also wrote longer things he thought of as novels. He couldn't sell them.

By 1979 he'd somehow passed himself off as a journalist and was publishing in top-shelf magazines like Playboy, Outside, Saturday Review, and Vanity Fair. In 1982, Shames was named Ethics columnist of Esquire, and also made a contributing editor to that magazine.

By 1986 he was writing non-fiction books whose critical if not commercial success first established his credentials as a collaborator/ghostwriter. His 1991 national bestseller, BOSS OF BOSSES, written with two FBI agents, got him thinking about the Mafia. It also bought him a ticket out of New York and a sweet little house in Key West, where he finally got back to Plan A: writing fiction. Given his then-current preoccupations, the novels--beginning with FLORIDA STRAITS--naturally featured palm trees, high humidity, dogs in sunglasses, and blundering New York mobsters.

ONE STRANGE DATE is the twelfth novel Shames has set in South Florida. While returning readers will encounter a couple of old friends, this new work can equally be enjoyed as a stand-alone.

To learn more, please visit http://www.LaurenceShames.com

WORKS BY LAURENCE SHAMES

Key West Novels—

Key West Luck

Tropical Swap

Shot on Location

The Naked Detective

Welcome to Paradise

Mangrove Squeeze

Virgin Heat

Tropical Depression

Sunburn

Scavenger Reef

Florida Straits

Key West Short Fiction—

Chickens

New York and California Novels—

Money Talks

The Angels' Share

Nonfiction—

The Hunger for More

The Big Time

Made in the USA
Lexington, KY
20 February 2017